WELSH ROSE AND HER LATIN LOVER

Could anybody be more prosaic, less romantic, less gallant and more constant than a solid Welsh socialist husband of ten years' standing? Why, only a forty-year-old Latin lover, of course. Rose Williams was not only married, Welsh, thirty and sensible, she was also in America on a scholarship to study Americans; but it was Giorgio, an Italian professor of International Law, who claimed her attention, who whisked her away in his convertible on a motel trip across the States. As we follow this strangely incongruous pair, quarrelling, coming together, travelling uneasily along electrically charged parallel lines, a wonderful real and delightfully comic picture emerges.

WELSH ROSE AND HER LATIN LOVER

Welsh Rose And Her Latin Lover

by

Anne Piper

Magna Large Print Books
Long Preston, North Yorkshire,
BD23 4ND, England.

British Library Cataloguing in Publication Data.

Piper, Anne
Welsh Rose and her latin lover.

A catalogue record of this book is
available from the British Library

ISBN   978-0-7505-3666-0

First published in Great Britain in 1961 by
William Heinemann Ltd.

Cover illustration © Wessel Wessels by arrangement with
Arcangel Images

The moral right of the author has been asserted

Published in Large Print 2013 by arrangement with
Anne Piper, care of Watson, Little Ltd.

Magna Large Print is an imprint of Library Magna Books Ltd.

Printed and bound in Great Britain by
T.J. (International) Ltd., Cornwall, PL28 8RW

For JOHN

But still for love the silly spirit pines
In searching for the logic of its dream,
In pacing endlessly those dark confines.

And so to every type love is a danger.
Some think it means no more than saying
  Yes,
And some turn canine when they reach the
  manger.

It seems a meaning we could hardly guess.

from 'Eighth Type of Ambiguity'*
JOHN WAIN

* Published in *Word Carved on a Sill* and reprinted here by kind permission of the publisher, Routledge & Kegan Paul, Ltd.

New York

Since neither of us had been long in America we did not know where to go to make love. It's not the sort of question you can ask a passer-by in a strange town ... or even a policeman.

'If we go to a hotel,' Giorgio said, 'they are at once asking for our passports. I had enough trouble to come here in the first place as my young brother is a communist.'

'We could get some luggage,' I suggested.

'All my luggage is very European ... they are asking more quickly still for passports when they see that. It is even possible adultery is illegal in the state of New York. A friend of mine was once arrested in Italy for kissing a girl in a car.'

'Anyway we don't have a car,' I pointed out.

We'd been walking too long and too far on a hot June afternoon, and now sat exhausted on a terrace in Central Park staring at a small pond. We were separated by a round iron table and two dirty coffee cups. Giorgio had not touched me for hours, my skin felt dry and too tight all over. I had slipped off my shoes and wondered if I'd ever get them back on my swollen feet. Giorgio mopped his damp face, he wasn't accustomed to all this walking either.

'Poor Americans,' he waved an arm at the energetic citizens rowing about in boats on the other side of the railing, 'that they have to call this a lake. If we were at Lago di Como now...'

'They do have big lakes ... up north.'

'Let us go up north then.'

'How?'

'When my licence comes ... then we can get a car.'

'Giorgio ... you know I can't leave the university now, not till the Seminar is over.'

'Of course you can leave, Rose. It is a big opportunity. I will take you all over the whole continent ... up to Canada ... down to Mexico ... across to San Francisco. It is not every day of the week a little housewife like you gets a Latin lover.'

'I don't have a Latin lover yet.'

I stared at the water some more. I didn't want one either if things went on like this.

'Next week I shall get some more money from the foundation,' he said. 'I am also arranging with them for educational travelling.'

I didn't like the sound of educational travelling. I started thinking about how I would go back to my room and wash my hair and do a bit of ironing and maybe write home and give up the whole idea of infidelity.

12

'Where is the country?' I asked idly. 'Couldn't we go there sometime in a bus?'

'Nobody goes in a bus in America.'

'But they must have woods and fields all the same?'

Gentle dark woods and soft secret fields lurking somewhere. I coaxed a drop of coffee along the table towards a dead match.

'Poison ivy.' Giorgio disposed of the country.

'The seaside then ... Manhattan's an island. We must be able to get to the sea somehow. I should like to bathe. How far is Cape Cod?'

Giorgio did not know. He had visited in White Plains, but seen no seashore there. He loosened his dazzling Roman tie.

'It gets hotter every day, Rose. I do not at all like it. We must go away out of this town very soon.'

'We could go round on the ferry boat.'

'Ferry boat? What good is that? I want to lie down – with you,' he added, as an afterthought. 'I am becoming ill. I have a headache.'

'Take an aspirin – I've got one.'

I fumbled in the bottom of my bag, and my fingers closed on the top of a melting lipstick. I drew them out messy and scarlet, but luckily Giorgio was looking the other way at a beautiful negress who moved between the tables to the door of the café. I wondered

13

again why he had ever looked at me. I have a pile of dark hair and blue eyes, but there is nothing remarkable about me ... at least not in Wales where I come from. I wiped as much red off my fingers as I could, and found the aspirin, but he had forgotten his headache. He scowled at me:

'I want a chocolate ice-cream, Rose. Ask for me, please.'

'But, Giorgio, you speak quite good English.'

'I don't like to. You ask.'

So I got up and went into the café and brought out his ice-cream on to the terrace.

'Why can't we go back to your place?' he asked with his mouth full. 'You know the old professor I stay with is not possible.'

'The Y.W.C.A. is not possible either, nobody brings lovers there.'

'How do you know? There are surely many fire-escapes. They should try. This is a free country, much freer than Italy ... it has no Pope, and sex is not the business of the President. Do you know in Italy you are not allowed to go up even to hotel bedrooms? You can go to prison for that.'

'Goodness me!'

'Of course we are kinder for tourists ... there is a notice in the university here for hospitality for foreign students ... I noticed it yesterday. You should go there and say, "I need a house. I have to *give* hospitality."'

14

'I never had a house ... ever since I was married we have always lived in rooms.'

Furnished rooms, other people's rooms with dark oak tables and slimy leather chairs, living like colourless gipsies, always moving on but without even our own painted caravan. Morgan does not believe in possessions. He gave away half our wedding presents, he will not even allow himself to become attached to a place, or a tree, or a view from a window. Once we had two rooms on the ground floor, with a little garden, only a *little* garden, but there was room for a washing-line and I grew a few herbs, mint and thyme and parsley. The clothes smelt so good that spring, drying out of doors after years of steaming round gas fires and dripping over cookers. But by the autumn Morgan was restless and we had to go.

'You Anglo-Saxons are barbarians,' Giorgio said.

'I am not Anglo-Saxon ... I am a Celt.'

'It is the same thing.'

'It is not.'

'Then the Celts are even more wild ... they had Tristan and Iseult. Now I am forty I need somewhere to sit down. A house, a good café with good *espresso* coffee, or my Alfa-Romeo. Come on, let's get out of here.'

'Where to?'

'The docks. I am thinking there must be facilities for sailors.'

15

'But, Giorgio, neither of us looks like a sailor.'

'Somewhere they don't ask for passports.'

He started to walk away very fast, his head down, his hands behind his back, his big Roman nose going ahead and his big black eyebrows drawn up together. He didn't even look back to see if I was following. He looked like that the first time I saw him, giving a lecture, walking up and down, caged by the small platform, using his arms a great deal as he talked, struggling with his bad English, beating it down physically into a shape he could bat across to us. Since the whole Seminar was made up of older people, post-graduates, foreigners like himself, we struggled with him to reach through to sense and none of us laughed. I had gone up afterwards with a question and then on out to lunch with him and missed the afternoon session that day and many afterwards. Now I had to run on my spindle heels to keep up with him. It was a strange seduction. But as I'd never been seduced before I didn't really know what to expect. I had no standards for sin.

'We will walk,' he announced.

'Oh, no ... but how far?'

'Five blocks, ten blocks.'

'Won't it be dangerous down there?'

'No more than in Central Park.'

'But perhaps the sailors have gangs and

rules about places and don't like foreigners coming?'

'It is reasonable that many of the sailors are foreigners, too. New York is a great port from all over the world. Do not be afraid.'

I was not really afraid of the sailors. I was afraid of what was happening inside me. Ten years I've been married now, since I was twenty, and never anything like this. Like what? 'I'm happy with Morgan,' I kept saying to myself. 'Morgan and I are very happy. We must be, we never quarrel, he is never angry with me, he is a very good man.' I tried to see him sitting there at the long table under the window correcting schoolbooks in the fading light. I could see all his single features clearly: he has a big nose too, and kind grey eyes, but although I could fix his eyes and his mouth even, and the nose, it didn't make a *whole* face, he hadn't any expression ... I couldn't make him lift his head and say, 'Rose Williams, don't do it. Get off Fifth Avenue and back to the Y.W.C.A. where you belong.'

'Why are you smiling?' Giorgio asked, looking at me suspiciously round about the Rockefeller Center.

'Thinking.'

'You should share all your thoughts with *me* now.'

'I was thinking about my husband.'

'Ah, no ... no need to tell me that. Forget

17

him. I do not like three people in one bed. He is a stupid man … very stupid … to let you travel alone and unprotected to America. I should never permit such a thing to my wife.'

'Morgan should have had the scholarship himself. He would not try for it.'

'I am not interested in him. Let us talk about me. Do you love me? Why do you not wear stockings?'

'Nylons are so hot.'

'Italian women always wear stockings in town.'

'American women don't always.'

'You should be elegant. You don't want to look like an American woman … but like yourself … you could be very nice if you try … a good Welsh woman.'

'With a pointed black hat?'

'Excuse me, please?'

'Never mind … there's a national dress in Wales.'

'What a horrible idea.'

But I didn't want to talk about national dress or any sort of dress. This walk through the canyons of New York was getting more and more like a bad dream.

'Giorgio … there's a blister coming on my heel. Couldn't we go to my doom in a bus?'

'If you have a blister it is because you are foolish and don't wear stockings. What is doom?'

'Sorry … joke … short for fate worse than death.'

'I don't understand you.'

'Never mind. Forget it. It wasn't important.'

We stood on the corner of 51st Street and looked for a bus. A great many hot and cross and tired New Yorkers seemed to be doing the same thing.

'I think it's their rush hour.'

'What is that?'

'The time when they all go home.'

'I should like to take you to my home now, Rose.'

'I don't think your wife would like that so much.'

'My wife is a very extraordinary woman.'

'I'm sure she is.'

'There is no room in these buses. *Andiamo–*'

He started to walk again, a little ahead of me. I wanted to hold his hand or even take his arm to make some contact between us, but he looked so stern.

'I thought Italians were supposed to be so romantic,' I tried breathlessly to keep up with him … 'and kiss people's hands and things.'

He turned round to look at me, but a man came between us and I couldn't hear anything.

'What did you say, Giorgio?'

'I? Nothing… What did *you* say?'

'I said I thought Italians were romantic – throwing roses–'

'Roses do not flourish well in Italy, we are not good gardeners, we are in too much hurry to wait for roots and all that growing to go on. Some are romantic, but many more are like I am, dry and cynical. What is the matter?'

'I'm tired.'

I stopped and leant against a bank, no wild thyme blowing, the Chase Manhattan, but it felt strong and cool with all that green money pressing against the walls. Giorgio kicked a grating, he didn't look at me. He seemed now to be cross with the traffic as well as the pedestrians.

'I too am tired,' he told a passing Pontiac, 'tired from wanting you.'

'I never knew it was so difficult to be wicked. I thought the primrose path was supposed to be easy.'

'You are never wicked before?'

'Well ... I'm selfish and lazy and...'

'My poor little puritan schoolmistress.'

'I told you I teach in the university now at home.'

'It is the same...'

'It is *not* the same ... we have better pay and longer vacations... And besides...'

'Do not be cross.'

'It's you who are cross, not me. I'm keeping quiet and calm.'

'Sh ... all these people will hear you.'

'I don't know them, and anyway I don't mind if they do, what's wrong with being calm?'

I struck the bank with my fist. I suppose I shouted, he touched me at last to soothe me a little, and we were both shaking. He had to take his hand away again and put it in his pocket. It did no good to either of us.

'We will soon lie down, Rose, and you will soon enjoy to be wicked, I promise you.'

'I have five dollars,' I said. 'Please, please, let's take a taxi.'

Giorgio looked at me as if I'd stolen it.

'You have five dollars? You stupid girl, why did you not say so before?'

'I don't know.'

'I told you you should share all your thoughts with me.'

'Five dollars isn't exactly a thought ... anyway haven't you got some of your own?'

'Also five-six dollars till my next cheque comes, but with eleven dollars we can do much better.'

He stepped boldly into the middle of the street, not waiting for the light to say WALK, stopped a yellow taxi and spoke to the driver. In the taxi I began to shiver, if only he would kiss me, claim me ... say he loved me or even, as my despair grew, liked me. So that I could feel smugly I'd been swept off my feet, carried into another world. All this free

21

choice was unbearable. I clasped my hands tightly in my lap. There was still time to jump out and run away. I did not understand why I, Rose Williams, was on my way to the waterfront with this tall dark handsome stranger who behaved as if the whole thing was inevitable, almost as if it had already happened. But it *hasn't* happened, and what do I know of him anyway? Afternoons crouched on stools in drug-stores chilly in the air-conditioning, mornings in the university feeling him shift restlessly when he had to be a student, when someone else talked of his work in some other country. Giorgio did not want to hear about other people's work. Then why did he ever come to America? What sort of happiness is he chasing? Did he foresee this taxi ride which I did not in my deepest dreams foresee? Anchored so safely so long in Morgan, I was only a boat out on a strong rope. For ten years I don't think I've even looked at another man that way even for a moment to wonder and want ... and now suddenly from my eyes to my toes I'm an aching emptiness of wondering and wanting. But I don't *like* him. I don't like him at all. He is selfish and easily bored and arrogant. I never want to see him again. I am going out of my mind. I'm out of my mind. Out of myself.

I put my hand to the door ready to jump when Giorgio stroked my cheek.

'You understand?' he said softly, speaking in French, it was our common language, I teach it. I have very little Italian, only what Latin leaves you with.

'No, Giorgio. Nothing. I'm not coming. It was all a mistake.'

I opened the door, but the taxi was stopping anyway. Giorgio pushed past me on to the pavement.

'I will kiss you later ... it is too soon ... I have, after all, still to walk a little way. Come.'

He pulled me out and held me firmly, all the time he paid the taxi. If he lets go of me I know I shall fall. The termites have been at my knees. Outside it didn't look like a hotel. No name or sign up over it, only a board which read 'Rooms – 6 dollars'. It was more than I paid at the Y.W.C.A. and not nearly so clean inside. The hall was badly lit with no carpet, only very worn linoleum. Giorgio, looking grimmer than ever but still holding on to my hand (I was far past running away now, my legs had gone soft), signed us in as 'Mr and Mrs Schmidt'. I don't know why, except that he particularly hates the Germans. Perhaps he thought they could shoulder a bit more of the world's guilt without noticing. They still come every summer and walk about in Giorgio's uncle's garden on the sea without being asked, so that they can show their wives their lovely gun sites. The

Italians prefer to forget about the war.

The surly man at the reception desk did not ask for our passports or our luggage. But he did insist on money in advance. The lift clanked very slowly up towards the tenth floor. The liftman had a mad zealous open face and wild white hair. The pile of books beside him on a stool had unexpected titles: *The Life of the Mahatma, The Way of Zen,* and *Lawrence in the Desert.*

'You folks staying long? Any time you want to borrow any of my books, let me say now, I am only too happy to lend them to you. You have any interest in the religious way of life? and by religion I don't mean organized church religion, none of that singing hymns on Sunday. I mean the good life, the good inner life when you don't tell the secrets of your heart to anyone, not to your dearest friend, not even your own husband or wife.'

'Excuse, please,' Giorgio murmured politely, coming back from far away at the word 'wife'.

'Not meaning any disrespect for your wife.'

'My wife is a very extraordinary woman.'

'I can see that, yes, sir, believe me; as soon as she stepped in my elevator I said, "Here's someone who is very close to the inner life, someone who has her feet in the true way ... the way to Nirvana."'

'Please, I think the elevator has stopped,' I pleaded.

'Why, so it has,' the liftman seemed surprised to have navigated the heights successfully. 'Must be the tenth then.'

He opened the gates with a flourish, crossed the passage and unlocked the door for us.

'I wish you folks a very good night,' he beamed kindly, without a suspicion of a wink, and shut us in.

'He was blessing us, Giorgio.'

'What was he saying? You should translate for me when you are making contact with the natives.'

'I don't think I was making contact. We had the wires crossed. I don't seem to make contact with anyone in this country.'

I sat down on the edge of the bed and slipped off my hot shoes again. Giorgio prowled round the room, opening cupboard doors and even peering under the bed and into the shower.

'What are you looking for?'

'In the fight against fascism I made many enemies.'

'Giorgio … I don't think your enemies could know you were coming here tonight. After all, you didn't know yourself ten minutes ago.'

His face lightened. He turned round and looked at me properly for the first time that evening and smiled, and I remembered why I had come. He smiled like that the first time we met, and the second and the third. He had only stopped smiling when the awkward question of love arose. Love seemed to make him very morose. Maybe Italian women arranged things better and always had empty marble palazzos ready. At least there was a big bed in this ugly little room.

'Now.' Giorgio took off his jacket briskly and put it on a hanger. 'Now we will turn the poor little schoolmistress into a woman.'

'I am a woman,' I protested as he began to remove the pins from my hair.

'Perhaps you pass for one in Wales.'

'But, Giorgio, if I'm so unattractive then why on earth…?'

'Be quiet … look – a river of night.'

He let my hair fall down over his arm. It comes to my waist. He stood back considering it, with a hairdresser's impartiality, as if he were wondering whether to cut it, wave it, or pile it up. He looks like a hairdresser himself with his own thick wavy hair, his great brown eyes, and his almost unbelievable good looks, but just as I decided that he was not only a hairdresser, but a totally strange hairdresser I'd never seen before, and that as soon as I got the strength back in my legs I'd go, he leant forward and began to kiss me, unzipping my cotton frock and slipping it sideways over my shoulders at the same time. He found the hooks at the back of my bra very quickly too, and soon I

26

was sitting on the bed dressed in my hair. I remember thinking it would have been pleasant to have a shower, it was a warm June evening and we'd walked a long way, and my feet were sticky and sore. I don't know how I thought things would turn out, perhaps that I'd have this cold shower, and then we'd lie down side by side, cool again, talking and kissing sometimes, and getting to know each other better, and being friendly, the way I am at home, but that wasn't the way it turned out at all. Two minutes after he'd got my hair loose there I was, flat on my back, fighting for my life. It seems sex is for strangers, not friends. I never knew lovers could be so cruel, that two people could be so close without any tenderness, I wanted to cry ... to cry out ... for help ... but help from whom? the liftman? ... but I couldn't get my breath for anything. There was enough light from across the street to see his eyes gleaming and I really wondered for a moment if he was going to kill me. People do get themselves killed like that, just by mistake. It would be a silly way to die.

But after a while he let me go, and then he said softly:

'Well ... so prim and self-controlled ... what are you thinking about? It's not like that in Wales, is it?'

'No,' I said, very dignified and unmoved, 'it's not, and I'm glad it's not, too. We have

27

more respect for other people.'

'Respect?' he said, and he began to laugh and he took my head in his hands and thumped it against the top of the bed.

'But that hurts,' I squeaked, really surprised and trying to rub it, but he had my arms pinned at my sides and as I struggled to free them and sit up he began to kiss my breasts and make love to me all over again.

Hours later, I was lying in a pool of my hair. I thought Giorgio was asleep, but when I started to edge away his arm clamped over me at once.

'What is it?' he mumbled.

'I want a drink.'

'I too ... a good whisky.'

'I thought water.'

'No ... no ... come.'

He switched on the light and we blinked at each other. He got out of bed and started pulling on his shirt.

'I thought we were staying the night here?'

'No, no, Rose. It is not a good place. It is the sort of place the police come. You can tell by the smell. They make enquiries. They find out I am here. There is trouble.'

'Do you think so really? Why should there be?'

'Yes. It is so dirty. Everything is dirty. I should never have brought you here. I have offended your puritan soul ... but my need of you was so great.'

'Why?'

'Why what?'

He was carefully knotting his tie.

'Oh, never mind.'

I went into the shower and turned it full on and altogether cold, so that it poured straight down and my hair was plastered to me, back and front. I couldn't make out what had happened. I mean, I knew what had happened in prose, in four-letter and longer words, but I couldn't make sense of it. I wish I didn't always have this urge to make sense and patterns, reasons and wherefores. I held out one arm and let the water stream over it. My hand looked the same, no dirtier and no more alive either. Giorgio walked in spruce again and ready to go.

'Be quick,' he told me. 'Why are you doing that? Now you are Ondine.' He handed me a towel. 'But you should not be ... now you must wait here till your hair dries.'

'I'll leave it down.'

'No. You are too old. It is not elegant in the street. You don't want to look like the dirty beat girls. You must put it up again to walk with me. But hurry, I want my whisky.'

'I'll put it up wet.'

I slipped a little and stumbled out of the shower. Giorgio walked back into the bedroom without holding out a hand to save me. Perhaps he didn't see. I bruised my thigh on the edge of the basin and felt a childish wish to burst into tears, to make more of my hurt, to have a focus for vague unhappiness. I dressed very quickly and pinned my hair tight on top of my head.

'I'm not going in that lift again.' I pulled Giorgio towards the stairs.

'Why not?'

'The man will tell me I've seen the inner light.'

'But perhaps he would be right and so you have?'

'No, Giorgio … no.'

'Soon I promise you … you'll see suns and stars.'

He took my hand and suddenly began to run with me down the ten flights of gaunt stone stairs. No one moved anywhere, no one came out of a door or stood on a landing or called the lift. Total grey silence round our clanging feet. I could not see how far down we had to go. It was like a prison. I began to share Giorgio's panic.

'Once I was in jail for a whole year,' Giorgio said as we ran. 'And three months alone … solitary confinement. I was only eighteen against Mussolini – Fascism. Since then I cannot bear to be shut in anywhere … not even a plane … always I must get out … out and be free. Sometimes at home I even get out of bed in the middle of the night to walk in the garden. We live in part of an old palazzo, you see, and the garden is very big … like an English park … full of old statues and nightingales and a few flowers. It is good for the children, they can play there and get lost. Just a little lost. I go to one temple and sit there sometimes till the dawn comes. My wife knows where to find me. She brings me coffee there in the first light. She has much patience with me.'

We slowed down to pass the reception desk and drop the key and then ran again in the street.

'Where are we going, Giorgio?'

My blister rubbed again.

'Uptown … to a good bar.'

'Why, look … it's only ten past ten.'

I had thought it might be tomorrow … or next year.

We clattered down into the subway and waited panting on the platform like a couple of hounded animals till the train came. We got into the front coach and stood in the rushing draught by a window. The wind beat on us, drying my wet hair, and the coach rattled ahead.

'We are safe,' Giorgio shouted, his face shining and happy. He hugged me and rubbed his cheek against mine.

'All is well. Do not be afraid.'

'I'm not,' I shouted, smiling too. Together we had escaped a great danger. He had not after all killed me.

Late that night in the Y.W.C.A., sitting up in bed in my right mind with my hair neatly braided, I wrote to Morgan. I'd been writing to him every day, but this time was different. I wanted to tell him everything, to have all the luxury of confession and never mind what he felt about it – to write, 'I've been unfaithful to you and it was terrible and I never will be again and I'm never going to see him again and I don't even like him and I realize now how good you are to me and always have been and I hate it here so far from home and I am wasting all the time I should be getting to know the Americans and seeing America and shall I turn right around and catch the next boat back?'

But of course I didn't say any of that. I told him about the fine United Nations building and the interesting discussion we'd been taken to there and the party at Giorgio's professor's house and how I was planning to go down to Washington for the week-end, and how I hoped again that Mrs Griffith on the floor below was really making him a decent meal, and how I wished he were there too. Then I looked around for more to say and watched the light winking on the top of the Empire State Building for a while, then I got out of bed and took the Christian Association's Bible off the top of the chest-of-drawers and shut it away where I couldn't see it. Not that I go to church any more myself, just Easter and Christmas for the singing, but the Bible is magic, old magic on its own. You've only got to open it anywhere and the great words come thundering out, you can be possessed by phrases for years like poor John Bunyan, and there's clouds of unknowing about where it may end.

The next day I stayed away from the university, and every day for a week. I didn't waste my time and my opportunities any more though. I bought a good guidebook and I went hard at the cultural sights of the city. I visited the Metropolitan Museum and the Guggenheim and the one for primitive art, and the Rockefeller Center and the Empire State and I took the boat-tour of the island and went up to the Bronx and down to Wall Street and Greenwich Village and everywhere I wandered in the music of the bells from the ambulances and fire-engines. So many and so often it's a wonder there are still that number of New Yorkers alive and well. They don't even raise their heads to a siren. When we were kids we were evacuated out of Cardiff up the Rhondda Valley, but we were in a few raids first and I still can't hear that siren, even for a factory dinner-hour, without a sinking in my stomach and waiting for the ker-rump of the bomb to come after.

I wore sensible, flat shoes and walked and walked. Twice Giorgio left notes with the hall-porter, he must see me, it was very urgent, but I tore them up and went on walking. I was getting very healthy with it.

Then one day I was eating lunch in the penthouse of the Museum of Modern Art, making a pattern with spilt salt on the good wood surface of the table, when I looked up and there stood Giorgio, and with him a very fine looking fair girl ... very young, too.

'Rose, I have been searching for you everywhere. Why are you not coming to your classes like a good student of America?'

He sat down without asking, and the fair girl sat down beside him and smiled kindly at me.

'This is Katrina,' Giorgio introduced us. 'Katrina from Denmark. She is helping me with my English. Why do you not help me with my English, Rose? You are speaking it better, even if you are Welsh. I do not think you have such a strong accent. You could be so good for me. When can we see each other?'

'Here I am, then,' I said, and I smiled too. It seemed easy to be polite. Giorgio looked over his shoulder as if he were still being followed. He lowered his voice and leant closer.

'No, no ... here there are too many people. We must speak together. I have many things to tell you. You should not eat those big

American sandwiches. They will make you fat.'

He took half off my plate and ate it himself.

'Katrina … go and get some coffee … for you also.'

Katrina got up obediently and went away.

'Poor Scandinavian women.' He watched with pleasure as she crossed the room in her tight skirt. 'They have the same sad time as American women.'

'You should not have spoken to her like that.'

'Why not? She likes it … she is a stupid girl and besides I have to talk to you alone.'

'I am not going to see you any more.'

I got it in very quickly and a little out of breath. Giorgio patted my hand.

'We have, all the same, to talk.'

'There is nothing to talk about.'

'We have to make plans.'

'What plans?'

'For our long trip across America.'

'I am not going across America … or anywhere, with you.'

'But I need you.'

'Katrina would be a much more suitable companion.'

Giorgio studied her across the room with the impersonal hairdresser's look.

'She has a beautiful body, don't you think, Rose?'

'I expect so.'

'Do not be so grudging. You can afford to be generous. You whose body has no rival. Don't you understand?'

'I don't understand anything.'

'Don't pretend to be stupid. You are not stupid like that poor beautiful girl. Love is always a matter of fantasy and for fantasy you must have intelligence. I should be bored with her by the time we are only at Pittsburgh. That is why I have decided to take you.'

I began to laugh. I laughed till I choked. Giorgio's soft eyes clouded with reproach.

'Rose ... I am not making a joke. I am altogether serious.'

'I know you are...'

I fumbled for my handkerchief. Giorgio passed me his.

'I'm sorry,' he said, 'it is not very clean. I find it very difficult in this democratic country to have a clean handkerchief. At home we have two maids, and a third who comes in only for the laundry. I wear clean clothes from head to toe every morning and my wife personally chooses for me my handkerchief.'

'There's nice for you,' I told him, wiping my eyes.

'So it's all settled. Tonight we have dinner together at my hotel, and this afternoon I buy maps of America.'

'So you have a hotel now?'

'But I told you ... my money has come. I have left the professor, everything is ready except you.'

'Well, I really hope you have a good time.'

'*We* shall have a very good time. You and I together.'

Katrina came back carrying the two cups of coffee carefully, not spilling any in the saucer. Giorgio swallowed his with one gulp and made a face afterwards.

'Why is American coffee supposed to be good?'

'It is ... by our standards,' I said.

'It's time you learnt, Rose, that for eating, drinking and making love your country has no standards. For gardens and government, yes ... for living – no.'

He stood up, jerked his thumb in the direction of the lifts and Katrina stood up too.

'He is going to help me choose a dress,' she told me. 'I am not very clever about clothes.'

'I am sure he has very good taste.'

'Then I buy the maps,' Giorgio said. 'And at seven-thirty, Rose, you come to my hotel.'

He had reached the lift before I realized he had not told me which hotel anyway. I began to laugh again, but quietly, inside myself, and then I saw him coming back, leaving Katrina waiting. He told me his address and his room number.

'I did not want Katrina to know where I am staying,' he explained, 'or she would be chasing me all the time. She finds me very attractive.'

'I'm sure she does, Giorgio,' I assured him, as solemnly as I could through my internal hysteria. 'You *are* very attractive.'

'Why are you wearing those ugly shoes?'

I glanced down at my comfortable sandals. I had thought them well concealed under the table.

'I've been walking a great deal lately.'

'Don't do it any more. You'll get thin. And tonight dress elegantly, and we will go out dancing.'

He jabbed his thumbnail into the back of my neck and walked off.

'I'm not coming,' I called after him. 'Ever...'

But he did not seem to have heard. At least he didn't turn his head. I watched him put his arm round Katrina's shoulders to guide her into the lift.

I went back to the Y.W.C.A. and lay down with my feet higher than my head. Everything I had felt about Giorgio had gone, it had been a fever, a short-time fever, it was something to do with being thirty in a strange country. Now I could with safety meet him again, not tonight, not this very evening in my best red silk, but sometime soon in a casual friendly way, perhaps at the zoo.

And I had learnt something too from the unfortunate, never to be repeated as long as I live, experience, he was right – I'd been too much of a schoolteacher before, too certain of right and wrong and good and bad and west and east. I had not made allowances for the sudden madnesses of the sane. For the rest of my virtuous life the edges of guilt would be a little blurred. I'd be gentler with the weaknesses of others, appreciate the different tones of grey. Trouble was, Morgan had no weaknesses. For ten years I had never known a time when he had not stood firm on all matters of principle, not that he was a prig, mind you, he liked people to be happy if they could, and enjoy themselves, but for all our friends he's always been the man of integrity. What does Morgan think? When Morgan left the party they all left, when Morgan went up to Aldermaston they all went, and always me just behind him too.

I sat up and wrote him a long letter about the Museum of Modern Art.

At about half past eight I began to feel a little hungry again ... perfectly normal, no loss of appetite, no loss of sleep. Any day now I shall even stop thinking about Giorgio ... so I went down to get a bit of supper at the drug-store round the corner. But I never got there because when I came out of the street door I heard a loud tooting and there was Giorgio in a big blue sports car, open roof, open shirt, silk scarf and all ... every inch the seducer.

'You are late,' he called cheerfully and climbed out.

'I told you I was not coming.'

'I did not hear you. Look ... *guarda che bella machina* ... is not she beautiful? I chose it only for you ... to match your eyes. It will suit us very well, I think. Come and look all around. Would you like to examine the engine?'

He opened it up before I could answer that I had never even mastered the principles of the combustion engine ... or the steam engine for that matter. And it is all very well to disapprove of nuclear fission but maybe one should be fair to the scientists and learn at least how to strip a bren gun or load a musket before stating firmly that one does not hold with death. But there's no time. If I went back to the bow and arrow now and worked up through the bloody centuries, I bet I'd still be stuck with that wretched horse in the Crimea drains (how did it ever get down the pipes in the first place?) when the twentieth-century strategists let go at last with their twitchy nerves and twitchy fingers and bring us to dust with all the other chimney sweepers.

'Is it very powerful?' I asked Giorgio, trying to look intelligently at the confused mechanism.

'Very.' He nodded his head reverently. 'We have a long way to go. Try the seat beside the driver. I shall drive all the time. It helps me to think. I have to write a book this summer.'

'I can't drive anyway. We've never had a car.'

'Now for supper I will take you to a good Italian restaurant I have found down near Washington Square. It is North Italian and the men go there and play in the bowling alley as they did in their town squares at home. I like it very much.'

I rooted my toes to the sidewalk.

'Giorgio ... listen to me ... just for one minute hear what I'm saying to you.'

'But I am always hearing what you say. You have a gentle voice. It is easier for hearing than women who shout. They should be shot.'

'You may *hear*, but you don't *listen* ... you just like the noise to run on while you think about something else.'

'And why not? I have many things to think about. It is very pleasant to have a woman telling of clothes and pretty things and what we shall have for dinner. I like that.'

'I don't even like you.'

I waited for him to look reproachful, but he only switched on the engine and said:

'Good ... good – then you will soon love

41

me. We do not want to be friends. Will you fetch your luggage now, or shall we return for it later?'

'I'm not going anywhere with you.'

I found myself stamping in a stupid ineffective way. You can't get a good stamp out of a high-heeled shoe. I wanted to kick the car. I said it again in French ... all of it, to make sure he understood.

'As you wish.' His voice was calm and uninterested. 'Then we will fetch it later.'

He leant across the pale blue leather and opened the door for me. I walked into the car at once furious, *furious,* with as much energy as if I had been going in the other direction. I banged the dainty blue door behind me still standing up, but as Giorgio let the car go at the same moment I fell forward and bumped my chin on the windscreen.

All my life I've been treated as a reasonable human being. I've been conditioned by reason and logic and good sense till I've become sensible. Maybe I was born sensible, at least I've always thought of myself that way. I'm a good teacher, and a good housekeeper, I manage my day very well. I organize my time constructively ... of course I should do, with no children and both of us earning, things have never been really hard. It was our parents who made the sacrifices. Morgan's anyway ... Morgan's father was a real old Keir Hardie type of socialist … he remembered sitting on Keir Hardie's knee as a child, and the old man telling him stories about India. Green parrots came to his mind whenever they talked of the old fighting days, but he saw to it Morgan got the best education going for a bright boy in the Rhondda. He pushed him and pushed him, and he sits there now coughing all day but pleased with Morgan. My father wasn't short of money, not for one child, but I can see now that he was very good to let me marry young without putting on a big lonely act to keep me by him. It would have been an easy blackmail, he could have made us go and live in his dingy old house with him, plenty of room there. But he was very brisk and practical, got himself a cheerful house-keeper and washed his hands of me with a good grace. Maybe he even likes it better like that … alone every evening and quiet, with his great big difficult jigsaw puzzles spread all over the dining-room table. The same view of highland horny cattle in a purple mist occupying him for weeks on end.

But I never learnt before how destructive it can be to take one step out of character, out of the charmed circle of your own idea of yourself. One rash move, and the rest of your ordered convincing life might as well never have been. I used to make jam every year, very good jam, no trouble with the pectin …

plum and greengage and strawberry, and marmalade too when the Seville oranges come in. Morgan likes a big tea when he gets back from school. And I always bottled fruit for the winter ... and pickles, and even salted beans. I wanted the food to be our own even if the furniture was other people's. Morgan doesn't notice what things look like in a room as long as he has people with him round the fire talking. He doesn't even mind if it's a gas fire as long as it's warm. I always washed his shirts myself and in ten years I must have darned thousands of pairs of socks ... but all those socks and shirts and jam and good sense weighed light in the scales, light as nuts in May, when Giorgio stopped the car on the way home from the Italian restaurant and slipped his hand into my cotton blouse and pulled me in close to him and began to kiss me.

I didn't even notice where we were till he drew away saying firmly: 'Now go and get your things.'

And I found we were sitting outside the open door of the Y.W.C.A. and the elderly man behind the reception desk could see us quite well. I got out and went in and up, and packed like a busy sleep-walker. I left one case in the basement, a small stake in the country. It took some time to do this because there was an old lady down there trying to get the negro night porter to weigh her trunk on a pair of small kitchen scales.

'If you ever want to come somewhere where nobody knows anything about anything at all,' she told me, 'come to New York.'

I don't know how the Christian Association usually save their young women, but they didn't do a very good job on me. Perhaps it's like youth hostels and they don't work on the over twenty-fives. I suppose I looked as if I could look after myself.

Pennsylvania

'Women subjected by ignorance to their sensations, and only taught to look for happiness in love, refine on sensual feelings, and adopt metaphysical notions respecting that passion, which lead them shamefully to neglect the duties of life, and frequently in the midst of these sublime refinements they plunge into actual vice.'
MARY WOLLSTONECRAFT.

In the car I put my head on Giorgio's shoulder and he drove slowly at first through the town with one arm round me. The roof was still down and I looked up at the dark and the shining tall buildings.

'Where are we going, Giorgio?'

'To the moon.'

'You are a very strange sort of professor. Do you behave like this at home in Italy?'

'Of course not. At home I am a very respectable citizen. I never go to the moon. It is not in the syllabus.'

'Not even with your students?'

'Particularly not with my students. That is why I like so much to chase the little girls here. It is a holiday for me. I shall not lose my job for it.'

47

'What did you do with Katrina?'

'Left her in Lord and Taylor's. She will be all right. Someone will soon find her. She was very beautiful, wasn't she?'

'Very beautiful,' very far away, a burnt-out star.

'It is sad there is not more time.' He sighed and kissed my forehead, waiting at a red light. 'But since time is limited I must choose the poor little mice like you who need love, and leave alone those who are strong by themselves and know that they are beautiful without any help from me.'

'Dear Giorgio ... you are so thoughtful and so generous.'

'Do not mock me. You will find this is true. You do not yet know your own strength, but through me you shall learn this and be grateful.'

'Perhaps through you I shall also learn about International Law?'

'God forbid that it should be necessary. I have never yet had a mistress who was interested in International Law. I keep that for my students.'

Once on the four-lane highway, Giorgio put both hands back on the wheel and drove with a speed which I tried not to notice. The flashing lights going by on the other side streamed into one silver ribbon and I slept for a while, waking to find that the moon turned out to be a castellated motel on the outskirts of Philadelphia.

This time the room was clean and pretty-pretty, with flounced pink bed-covers and frilly lampshades, but Giorgio went through his anti-fascist prowling routine again in and out of the cupboards and the bathroom.

'I don't like that at all,' he growled, kicking the twin beds, so that the flounces shook.

I sat down on one of them.

'I'm very tired,' I yawned truthfully. 'Perhaps we could both just go to sleep tonight?'

'Alone? In two separate beds? You English are mad ... you come all this way to commit adultery and then you want to make everything cold and comfortable like an old dull marriage... What is the matter with you? You are not even ill.' He glared at me as if he hated me.

'I'm not English.'

'It is the same.'

'Stop saying everything is the same ... things can be different even if some of us are unfortunate enough to be born outside Italy ... we can't all be part of the Holy Roman Empire.'

He hung his jacket up and shut the cupboard.

'It is true ... it is not your fault ... my poor little puritan mouse ... if your blood runs cold.'

There was nothing to throw at him, un-buttoning his shirt, except a map of Penn-

sylvania, so I threw that. It was not heavy
but the corner got him in the eye so that he
came at me with his head down and blinking. He knocked me across the two beds
sideways so that the gap between them was
in the small of my back.

'Giorgio, don't ... I didn't mean to hurt
you. I'm sorry ... don't tear my blouse ...
it's so stupid ... just because I'm tired...'

He dragged at the buttons and one flew
off.

'And I haven't even got a needle and
cotton. I can undress myself. You're hurting
me... Oh, what do you want me to do...'

He wrenched the blouse off and threw it
on the floor over my head.

'Always talking ... always explaining, stop
being neat and tidy and mending your buttons ... stop thinking ... start to feel with
yourself, all of your body ... here and here.'

Now he was breaking my shoulder straps
as well.

'Let me at least take my shoes off,' I
screamed, getting my knee up into his stomach. To my surprise he fell back gasping. I
sat up and looked down at him. His face
had gone yellow.

'What's the matter?'

'My liver ... it is swollen ... I have to take
great care.'

'Oh, dear ... I'm so sorry ... but why didn't
you tell me?'

'How could I know you were going to be so brutal and kick me when I am only offering you my love? My wife would never have done such a thing.'

'You probably never fell on your wife like a mad bull.'

'I once tried to strangle her in my sleep,' he smiled proudly at the memory.

'You did? Why?'

'Poor woman … she was with child at the time, too … I was dreaming. I had a bad dream that the fascist guards were attacking me … five of them, and all I had was my bare fists … they were armed – everyone with machine-guns – so I thought they are come now to kill me but I will kill at least one of them tonight before I die, so I leap and I get my arms around just one neck, and I squeeze – so – and after all it is only my poor wife screaming, *"Mamma mia!"* Her mother was in the house with us at the time on account of the soon birth of the little baby. She was a very beautiful little baby with fair hair.'

'I'm glad,' I loosened his hands nervously from my throat. 'Do you often have this bad dream?'

'Not so often and now my wife knows what to do.'

'Oh … and what does she usually do?'

'She tickles me … I am very ticklish … if you wish you may tickle me.'

'I'll wait, thank you. I'll wait till the strangling starts.'

'Now you are angry with me.'

I got up and took out my nightdress and went into the bathroom to wash. Here I am cleaning my teeth, just like I always do, and nothing is changed. I let my hair down, brushed it out and then plaited it back again, just like I always do with a last twist of a rubber band to keep it tight.

I took one pink bed-cover, folded it and laid it across a chair. I couldn't fold the other one as Giorgio was still heavy on it, groaning slightly. He had moved round a little so that his head was on the pillow. His eyes were shut and he looked a little yellow. I wondered if I ought to get a doctor for him. I got into my bed and turned over towards him.

'I really am sorry, Giorgio. Is the pain better now?'

'A little.'

He reached for my hand with his eyes shut and laid it approximately on his wounded liver.

'You should not have been so rough with me, you know. Do you see, Giorgio? It was the wrong thing to do ... tearing me about like that ... after all, I am a human being.'

He drew my hand down lower.

'I, too, am human ... feel how much I love you even when I am suffering. You should be good to me. Please be good to me.'

I examined the pitchpine ceiling, from my pillow. I tried to make a pattern of the knots like the muscles in an anatomy diagram; perhaps if I kept entirely still, not even moving my fingers, this strangely alive restless Giorgio would doze off. Tomorrow morning I would take a train back to New York and no harm done. With my free hand I could even now be getting on with my letter to Morgan, except that it was still shut in the case over by the door. Giorgio seemed to be breathing heavily, he must have gone to sleep. I drew my right hand a little away from him, but he opened one eye at once. To my astonishment this eye literally sparkled, no sign of any recent suffering.

'Have you taken off your shoes yet, Rose?'

'You know I have … why, you were only pretending.'

'No, I was not. I was very ill, now I am well. You have felt how well I am for you. Now you will feel me better.'

He rolled over, pulled away my sheet and took me in his arms.

'I like this little slippery petticoat, I have to guess you.'

'It's not a petticoat. It's a nightdress.'

'Never mind what it is. I like you to wear it … and I like also very much to take it off. Look how you are starting out rosy towards me like two little shrimps. Shall I eat them up? You see, you too are ready for me. You cannot help that. Don't be frightened … we shall be so happy together. Let yourself be warm. You are a very difficult woman. Why have you caged up your poor hair all again? At night it must be free to breathe, or it won't shine for you.'

He tugged at the rubber bands round my plaits and tears came into my eyes as he pulled and untwisted.

'Don't cry. I am not hurting you … only loving you. You need so much love. You are a thirsty plant in a dry place, a rose in the sand. Only let yourself be warm. You should be soft like your hands – when you were holding me just now so gently. I trusted myself in your hands … trust me in you … let your heart be all soft for me also.'

'I'm not crying. You hurt my head pulling my hair.'

He kissed my eyes and my hair.

'Be brave … it was only a little, and with your hair loose you can forget the school. All the schools … for far too long. Now take me, love me.'

'Oh, Giorgio.'

'That is better … say my name again … very soft like that.'

'Giorgio…'

'My English Rose.'

'Not English.'

'It is the same…'

54

Everything is the same … English, Scots, Italians, Welsh, Eskimos, Americans, all struggling together with hope and with passion, in motels and igloos and log cabins and marble palazzos. A marvellous sweetness steals over them all, a sugar coating to the summer … nothing behind but fruit and jam … nothing ahead but nights and nights of molten joy.

In the morning Giorgio was cross. I drew back the curtains to let in the sunshine. I was still surprised then by the sun. It is so often raining in Wales and particularly in the summer.

'Oh, look, Giorgio … it's a lovely day.'

'Don't do that,' he growled. 'Get me a fruit juice.'

I pulled the curtains to again, disappointed that he would not share the weather with me, and opened the front door to look for a café.

'Come in at once,' Giorgio called, using one eye again. 'You should not be seen like that.'

'I have my coat on.'

He opened the other eye as well and scowled.

'But your legs are bare. Get dressed and use the telephone. We are in America now.'

I didn't think it necessary to dress for the

telephone, so I shut the front door and sat down on Giorgio's bed. As I lifted the receiver he pinched me, very hard.

'Ow...' I yelled at the operator.

'Can I help you?' asked the girl politely. She put me through to the restaurant and I asked for breakfast.

'What did you do that for, Giorgio?'

I moved carefully away to the other side of the room.

'You looked so prim.' He wound the sheet round his head like an Arab. 'I wanted to see your expression.'

'But it hurt ... it wasn't just playful... What's the matter with you?'

'What's the matter with you, Rose, that you make such trouble about being hurt? It is so much part of life ... more natural than joy. You must never be afraid of pain.'

I began to twist up my hair.

'There is enough pain in the world anyway without causing any more.'

He grinned at me, not using his eyes. I could see him in the glass.

'Ah, but think,' he sighed, 'of the happiness of causing pain to a loved one.'

'You're mad,' I mumbled with my mouth full of pins.

'No. It is you who are still too sane, my darling. We must alter that. You are missing so much. As your hair goes up on top of your little head so your scruples are stif-

56

fened. Today you are planning to leave me.'

'How did you guess?'

'I can see it in your backbone. It is a very fine backbone. It tells me everything.'

I faced round to him.

'It would be better if I went ... we don't understand each other at all. We aren't the same sort of person. I'm not right for you, and this isn't right for me, either. I mean, it may be an ordinary thing for two married people in your country, but it isn't for me ... we can get divorced and you can't. I expect that alters the situation and...'

'Come here.'

It was foolish to go anywhere near him. As soon as he could reach me he put out his arms and pulled me over him and my hair all came down again. I lost a pin in the thick dark hair on his chest. It would have been more romantic to deck him with those old forget-me-nots. But there were no wild flowers to hand and no rain to run out into. He squeaked as I began to search and tickled him.

'What are you doing to me like a mother monkey?'

'Trying to find my hair grip ... honestly, you ought to do something with all this ... turn it into an industry ... nice for rugs.'

'Do not insult my strength with talking of rugs.'

'Found it...'

I tried to sit up, but he held me to him tighter than ever.

'Giorgio ... no ... not now.'

'Why not?'

'Because ... oh, because lots of things... It's the morning, it's broad daylight ... I don't know you in daylight, and besides I'm almost dressed.'

'It is time you know me in daylight. You have no train to catch, no need to go to a school. We have all day to love. Kiss me.'

I kissed him quickly on the forehead.

'No, not like that.'

Someone knocked loudly on the door.

'Giorgio ... let go ... don't be silly.'

'They will go away.'

Another knock ... getting more impatient.

'No, they won't ... it's the coffee.'

'Coffee?' He let me go. 'I said fruit juice. Why did you not get me fruit juice? I cannot drink coffee in the mornings with my liver. You must learn how to please me.'

I paid for the two paper bags they handed over and put them down beside Giorgio, but by the time I drank the coffee it was very cold and tasted strongly of cardboard container.

'I must know,' I said sternly, as I put my hair up for the second time, 'where we are going.'

'We go like the wind ... wherever we feel like.' He spread his arms to embrace America.

'No … more precisely … I must have an address somewhere, sometime I must send a cable to Morgan. I can't just disappear. I am a person. I have a life I belong to.'

'Do not be so practical.'

'But he would worry.'

'Let him worry … he will love you more.'

'No, he won't … you don't know him. He's not like that.'

'How do you know what he is like?'

'I've been ten years with him.'

'And he beside you … and what does he know of you?'

I tried to imagine Morgan with a kept woman in Barry. But he is always so very busy, there are so many political meetings. I know they exist because I am so often there, too. He doesn't say, 'Darling, I'll be late back from work tonight' … he says, 'Don't forget Ben is expecting us both to turn up at his branch meeting.' And turn up we both do. What am I doing here now this fine June morning?

'Oh, Giorgio … say somewhere, please … somewhere that'll be on the route for sure.'

He pushed back the sheet and stretched.

'Tell him Santa Fé. I am going down the Santa Fé trail … for the sake of my little son, I must see the cowboy country.'

'How old is your son?'

'Janni is eight years old. He is always very interested in cowboys. I must bring him something of the Indians also. He is a very beautiful boy ... and always cheerful ... it is remarkable. The two girls are often quarrelsome, screaming, pulling each other's hair, taking away toys, but Janni is like sunshine in the house, always laughing, never any need to scold him. Sometimes I give him a little smack to remind him that life cannot always be so easy for him as now, but he only kisses me and says, "Papa is joking."'

'Oh, yes.'

'You see, he understands me. He has patience with me.'

'I don't see any reason why I should take part in this conspiracy to humour you.'

'Why not? You would be happier like that.'

He went into the bathroom and left me before I could think of a dignified answer. When he came back he said:

'Why don't you pack my things?'

I looked round me at his things thrown all over the room. He had not used them, but pulled everything out in order to get at his razor which must have been pushed down to the very bottom.

'I'd better start at the beginning. You are in a muddle.'

'That is the best,' he agreed. 'My wife always packs for me. She is very good at that. She will not even let the maid touch anything. If I cannot help you I will go out and buy a newspaper. We should know what

60

is happening in America. We are here for that.'

He had one last look at his well combed hair and left me.

I laid all his clothes out on a bed and made some sort of system. It was a relief to be able to make a system out of anything, even socks. I had a drifting idea that if I could only organize the socks I could organize my emotions too ... shoes and socks and home life at the bottom, then a nasty collection of dirty hankies and hurt prides and resentment, with aertex underwear and honesty, and silk shirts and the delicious flattery of being wanted, higher up, and his razor, for putting an end to everything metaphorically, easily found near the top. I could so easily get out of it, easily go, easily take the train, only two hours back to New York and the decently cultural visits. The silk shirts worried me. They would soon be too hot for Giorgio to wear. He'd be changing them all the time and then who was going to iron them? He wasn't the sort of man to wear an unironed shirt.

Giorgio didn't come back for an hour. I had plenty of time to pack my own things, send a cable to Morgan, finish my letter to Morgan, file my nails, read up Philadelphia in the guide-book, and think heavily about that train to New York, before Giorgio reappeared whistling the Red Flag and without a newspaper.

'Where have you been?' I asked, sulky and querulous.

He frowned at me, as if seeing me clearly for the first time that morning.

'You are not my wife to ask that sort of question.'

'I only asked...'

'I must be free to come and go as I please.'

'It seemed a long time to NOT buy a newspaper in.'

'Excuse me?'

'You didn't buy a paper?'

'Did you want a paper?'

'*You* wanted one.'

'No. I had my shoes cleaned. Are you ready now at last?'

'I've been ready for half an hour.'

'Do not look so displeased. It does not suit you. It spoils the splendid tranquillity of your classic face. You must always be smooth and calm. Like a deep lake. Now we will leave here, where shall we go?'

'We ought to stop in Philadelphia. The book says there are several fine old churches.'

'I was brought up in Rome. I did not come to America to see old churches.'

So we shot through Philadelphia and up on the Pennsylvania Turnpike into rolling green country with plum-red Dutch farms and big black barns. Giorgio drove very fast, faster than the Turnpike speed limit, he didn't think much of the Turnpike speed limit. Cars in Italy, though smaller, went much faster. He did not see the point of having this powerful motor under his hands if he couldn't make it roar. It was already too hot to have the roof down and he turned on the air-conditioning. He was very pleased with this gadget and turned it on and off several times so that blasts of draught whipped my legs and away again.

'Magnificent ... cold air and the ice blue windows.'

He at once wound down a window to look out and see what colour the country really was. As he was wearing dark glasses anyway the window can't have made much difference. When I pointed this out to him he took off the glasses as well, and the car swerved towards a Greyhound bus.

'Giorgio, look out,' I screamed. 'Mind the bus.'

'Why did you tell me to take off my glasses?'

'I thought you could see without them.'

'I have very poor sight. You should know this.'

'But you hardly ever wear glasses.'

'They hide my eyebrows ... which are very fine...'

'Giorgio ... but you're a man.'

'That you should know now, too. Why so scornful, anyway? Men also should look

63

beautiful … to give pleasure to others.'

'Oh, I don't know … it seems kind of silly… Oh, do look at the road now anyway and forget about your eyebrows. There's a great trailer coming up behind with most of a house on it.'

'I know. I can see. You worry too much. Relax. You are with me.'

I dropped my hands and closed my eyes.

'Don't worry, girl,' Morgan said. 'You are with me.'

'It's quicksands,' I said. 'Must be … where are all the people then?'

'Too early … to get themselves out from Milford Haven. Look at the gulls there walking safe.'

Delicate webbed feet walk anywhere, even on the water.

'Oh, Morgan, wait … if we had webbed feet now.'

And he laughed and left me to sit on the top of the cliff while he went down to bathe alone. He turned and waved to me as he walked hard across the dangerous sands and swam out to sea. I was ashamed then to be so afraid and let him go like that, and I blushed sitting up there too far away even for the gulls to see, and I climbed down the path and was waiting at the water's edge with his towel when he ran out shaking the sea from his ears and out of breath, and he swung me off my feet and shook me in his wet arms and said:

'Now you are married there are a lot of things you must learn to take on trust... Now let's get back to the farm. I'll want two eggs for breakfast today.'

The ripe cornfields dipped to the edge of the blue sea. We lay in a sheltered hollow with so many plans to keep us company. Labour would win this election, too, in 1950.

'We've only begun,' Morgan said. 'There's so much still to do. People must see ... they *will* see ... give us fifteen years' socialism and they won't know the old place. It's a good time to live, Rose, with work and a future at last.'

'We'll have a family, won't we, Morgan? Two of each.'

'Later – later ... you're so young, Rose ... I don't want you tied to all that washing and backache and misery yet. The way I've seen my mother go.'

'But you said a time for work.'

'There's other work ... you can be with me all the time ... I need help.'

'Couldn't we have one baby? Just a small one?'

I tickled his chin with a piece of grass, but he was not to be distracted.

'Maybe the next ten years will even see Nye get to the top – we'll have fireworks then all right. What do you say?'

'I say I want a little house with a little front door and a little baby in it.'

'Baby yourself, only just out of your teens. I don't mind a child bride – but I don't want a child mother as well … you think about *me* for a while. Time enough for babies. Look at that lark now resting his song on the sky. There's beauty for you–'

'Couldn't we go somewhere beautiful?' I asked Giorgio.

'We will make beauty … wherever we go.'

That night we made beauty in a motel beyond Pittsburgh. But first we ate crackers, soup and hamburgers on the road.

Giorgio glowered at his chunky hamburger.

'I want wine,' he said to the surprised boy behind the counter.

The boy shrugged hopelessly and turned to me. So did Giorgio.

'Get it,' he commanded us both.

'Giorgio, no … we are in the wrong place.'

'I need wine with this terrible food.'

I explained to him about drug-stores and bars and the boy offered him coffee.

'Too much coffee in this country … too many people awake and nervous … let us have a good English cup of tea.'

But there was no tea either and Giorgio began to eat with enormous angry bites.

'Don't eat so fast,' I said.

'Don't tell me what to do.'

'I only thought it might be bad for you ... give you indigestion.'

'Stop thinking what is good for me.'

'But, Giorgio, you are always saying what is good for me.'

'The difference is I *know* what is good. Your hair is coming down. Pin it up properly.'

I went away to the rest-room feeling I was coming to pieces all over. My nose shone in the evening heat, my nylon slip was proving too airless for American summers. I splashed some tepid water on my crumpled face, and then saw through watery lashes there was no towel, only a hot air machine for drying hands. I crouched down and tried to get my face in line with it and ended up scrubbing around with a piece of Kleenex. I looked worse than ever. If it's worth doing it's worth doing well; even running away, I was beginning to understand, needed practice. You did not just give up ... abandon was not all. I would have to work at this new life too, and there are no textbooks on how to do this, even if I had time to read them.

Why was Giorgio so cross all day, for a start? It seemed to me, looked at logically, I was the one to be cross. In fact, I had a right to be *very* cross. He had dragged me out into the middle of nowhere (Pittsburgh must be the centre of many people's lives and who am I to belittle the steel industry? But it seemed like nowhere to me) only to insult me. He clearly didn't like the way I looked, the way I spoke, the way I moved. Why the hell didn't he leave me behind? How dare he treat me so badly, he has no rights over me, I am entirely free.

I put on a lot of lipstick and marched bravely back into the café all ready to say: 'Giorgio ... I'm going ... I've had enough.' But he wasn't there. I'd left him sitting on a stool by the counter hunched over a glass of freezing milk. The glass was still there, only half empty, but no Giorgio. I walked down the line twice to make sure. There wasn't a single face I'd ever seen before. A fat man, a thin young man, an old woman, a young woman trying to feed three children at once ... all strangers. By this I establish that Giorgio is not a stranger. I may not know him, but at least I know him a great deal better than these occupied Americans. He has broad shoulders and a broad stomach and his eyebrows jut out almost as much as his nose ... and he's not HERE. He's gone ... he's taken all my clothes and driven off and left me to drown. He has tired of me by Pittsburgh, as he said he would of Katrina. He's bored with my nagging, my ordinary face, my lack of experience. One dull night with me was enough. I should never have criticized him, argued with him, rearranged his packing. Italian women are gentle, sweet, submissive, elegant, and how had I ever dared to hope he might love me?

'Where's he gone?' I asked the boy behind the counter.

I was out of breath with fright. The boy shrugged his shoulders, a different boy in any case.

'Where's who gone?' He swept away the half-glass of milk.

Surely I wasn't away so long as all that? Not like that princess in the fairy story who went out on the balcony for a minute and came back to the ball to find a thousand years had passed. Don't say you have to keep time turning besides everything else and that if you put a foot wrong you are going to slip sideways into another century as well. But glad we should all be to find there *is* another century not so different from the last after all. But glad I altogether am not to find myself alone in, or nearly in, Pittsburgh.

I pushed my way out into the warm darkness, tears furred the lights for me, but even so I could see him standing on the corner of the street, examining a parked Cadillac.

'Oh, Giorgio...'

I rushed at him like a lunatic and fell into his arms. He staggered but braced himself against a house and shifted the toe I was standing on.

'What is it, my little one?' he asked, quite kindly, considering the pain I must have caused him.

'Oh, Giorgio,' – you exist, you are solid and here and not skulking in another cold century. Your heart beats, you don't even complain that I am leaning on your liver.

'I thought you'd gone ... I thought you'd left me... Oh, Giorgio!'

I clung to him, drowning with relief this time. He stroked the back of my neck absent-mindedly, as one might an insistent dog, still looking at the car over the top of my head.

'But what is it, then, Rose? You don't love me, so no matter if I go away from you.'

'But I do ... I do. I didn't know. I didn't know it was like this, so much pain and anger. Why can't you be kind to me? It seems to me so easy to love...'

'Easy?... It is the most difficult thing in this world. You talk as if you have some right to love ... as if love were like higher education or better housing ... can't you see love comes to one in a million? It is not likely it will come to us. It is not to do with sex or marriage or from which country you come ... it is who you are. Whether you have a talent for it or not. It is like perhaps the Catholic idea of grace ... you have no right to it, but if it comes it descends on you from the sky like an extra benediction. Even the Americans with their wonderful Constitution only have the right to *pursue* happiness. No one can guarantee they'll catch it up, however fast they drive the Cadillac down the four-lane highway.'

'It's less than love I hoped for … I wanted kindness.'

He put both hands round my neck and rocked me towards him.

'You are a stupid woman. How can you be so old and so innocent? What do they do to you over there in the rain? Come quickly. I prefer my Alfa Romeo at home to this Cadillac. We will stop at the very first place we come to with beds. I think there is only one way you and I can understand each other.'

That motel had a pink ceiling, but Giorgio turned the light off as soon as he had hung up his jacket neatly.

'Oh, talk to me, please,' I pleaded.

'Not by talking … it is no good … understand with your body.'

'But I don't know how.'

'I am showing you.'

'Tell me in Italian.'

'French is a good language for love.'

'But I want to hear what you sound like *really* … when you are at home. French is pretending for both of us.'

'Love has much pretence. It must always be created. Otherwise you are only an animal.'

'Say it once in Italian.'

'I have more respect for my wife than to say *"Ti amo"*.'

'Is that how you say it? *Ti amo?*'
'You sound stupid. Don't speak Italian. You have a very bad accent.'
'But, Giorgio ... I only wanted to learn ... to learn your language to be closer to you.'
'Be quiet ... that is not the way...'

Kansas

Giorgio was pleased with Kansas.

'This is what I came to see.'

He stopped the car by the side of the road and got out, and we stood side by side under the hot sun in wide dry emptiness. Flat, flat grey-green land stretched to the sky north, south, east and west. In the far air a silver grain storage building rose like a mountain in the way a single church gives meaning to the flatness of Holland.

'In Italy we have nothing like this ... even south of Naples we are aware always of so many human beings scratching and struggling to live.'

'There are empty parts of Wales. But they are hills, up and down, sharp and green and stony.'

'You should come to Italy.'

'You should come to Wales.'

'Excuse me ... I think not.'

In Kansas City we read warnings of a tornado. Giorgio got very excited. He wanted to chase the tornado out on to the plains.

'No – please ... it might turn on us and kill us.'

'Never ... it goes only along one side of the

73

street whipping up all the houses. I should like very much to see that.'

'But we might be on the wrong side of the street.'

'You can see it coming and cross over. It is a pillar of fire. Like Moses in the wilderness.'

'Smoke, I think ... or dust, rather.'

'I think fire. In any case we have nothing like that in Italy and I should see it to tell my son. But first I must go to the post office.'

'But how would anyone send you a letter here?'

'Because I tell them to, of course.'

'But if you knew we should come here, why didn't you *tell* me?'

I felt like thumping on his closed face.

'It is more romantic not to know where you are going...'

'Romantic ... but you don't believe in romance ... you do your best all the time to destroy ... anyway, damn you, I wanted to *know*...'

'Only to tell your husband.'

'But of course to tell my husband ... why not? Why can't I have a husband same as you have a wife?... You are all the time secretly telling her where you are.'

'That is different.'

'What is different, for goodness sake?'

'I have the children to think of ... I must look after the little children, and my wife also. She is very unhappy without me. She is accustomed that I do everything for her. Now she must make the long journey from Rome to the sea alone, with only the domestic to help her.'

'But...'

But your culture is not my culture, your life is not my life, and each glimpse I have of it puts me further away. I shut my mouth and followed him down the street.

We waited a long time in the busy post office. First at the wrong counter. Giorgio made me stand in front of him and do the talking, as usual he acted as if he were deaf when an American spoke to him saying, 'Excuse me...' and, 'You tell them, Rose.'

In the end we discovered he had three letters.

We sat in a drug-store while he read them and I drank two cups of coffee and watched a gentleness I had never seen before on his face.

'See what he says, my clever son.'

He threw one letter across the table. I could not read the Italian, but I examined the drawing of a hulking Noah's Ark on a tiny green sea.

'What does he say?' I asked.

'Excuse, please?' He looked up, angry again at the interruption.

I pointed at the child's letter.

'I don't understand what he says.'

75

'He says, of course, that he is unhappy without me. They are all unhappy without me. He draws a picture of the boat which will soon bring me back home to them.'

He went on reading the letter from his wife.

'She has not started yet for the seaside ... Anna, the second girl, is not well. When was this sent?' He peered at the postmark. 'Maybe she has the measles. She has trouble also with my brother who comes to borrow money. Poor woman, and also the girl who comes for the laundry is ill, and the second maid must do the washing. What confusion. It is all very difficult. How can she manage?' He turned the page. 'Ah ... now it is better. Anna is better, her fever has subsided, they will start in a few days, but my wife must drive the car for four hours, she has never been so far without me before. Perhaps the car will break up.'

'Down ... break down.'

'Why should it?'

'I don't say it *should*. I mean, if it did that's what you'd call it. Anyway, there must be garages everywhere ... even in Italy.'

'She has to drive through wild mountain districts before she comes to our part of Liguria.'

'I expect she will be all right.'

He drew his eyebrows together and looked at me sternly.

76

'You should be able to consider the problems of other people.'

'Yes, Giorgio.'

'Not always wrapped up in your own pleasures.'

Pleasure is it now? Whatever next–

'No, Giorgio.'

'You must not be jealous of my wife because she has children.'

'No, Giorgio ... of course not.'

'Why do you not have some children? Every woman should have children. You have the body of a young girl, at your age it is not right. It is indecent that your body should have no character, no marks of living and suffering. You should ask your husband to give you a child before it is too late.'

'Morgan wants children. At first we were too poor, and now they don't come.'

He bowed politely across the table.

'My commiserations, madam. You should relax more. But perhaps you are sterile? My wife is very fertile, and since she is also Catholic we have always to be careful.'

He lost interest in me again as he started reading the third letter. I walked out and stood stupidly in the hot street with a glaze of new tears between me and the city. I will not cry again. I will not become red-eyed and desperate. I leant my forehead against a plate-glass window, but it was not cool. One gets homesick for stone in America, cold

cold stone. There must be stone buildings somewhere, but I never saw them. Come to that, I've never seen the Tower of London either. I remember a stone tower half buried in sand near Llantwit Major. Sand groping in from the shore, drifting like snow between the pine trees long out of sight of the sea. Stone walls in Cornwall might be hiding the sea too, and stone farms in the Cotswolds built on sheep and the sheep above Machynlleth rubbing their sides on stones.

'What are you looking at?' Giorgio asked, putting an arm round my shoulders.

What am I looking at? Sheep and stones. I looked to see.

'An ice box,' I said.

'You should not look at things without me, we will look at America together. Together we will write a little article. I will have the ideas on ice and sterility in America, and you will help me with my English. We shall publish it first here in the *New Yorker*, and afterwards in a Roman paper, perhaps *Il Mondo?* In this way we shall pay our trip. What do you say? Perhaps I shall write a book about American women as we go along.'

'Do you know any American women?'

'Naturally. In New York anyway. My professor's wife, the secretary at the Foundation, a Mrs Schnell who asked me several times to her house.'

'Did you go?'

78

'Not yet … but I saw that she also was very sad. American women are always very sad when they see Italians, it reminds them how much they are missing all the time in life with their husbands who bring home the groceries and do what they are told until the day they have ulcers and are no good any more.'

'What's the difference between ulcers and a bad liver?'

'What is the matter, Rose? You look sad also. And too hot.'

'It *is* too hot. I've never been as hot as this in my life before.'

'Let us go to a bar and have a good whisky with many rocks, it is not your fault, my rain maiden, if you are melting away in the sun, and after all I love you.'

'Do you?'

I turned to see if it could possibly be true, but those limpid eyes could be read in any way … any way in the world. Who ever claimed that eyes expressed emotion? Eyes, even above a yashmak, can do nothing on their own but stretch and shrink like thought moving through a cat, and people can say it and say it and talk and kiss till the tongue aches, but you can never know what saying it means.

He laughed at my solemn searching face and rubbed my nose.

'Of course, yes … or you would not be

here. I will not love you very much or very long … I cannot risk such a thing … but it is enough for now, don't you think? Enough to make us happy together?'

'Giorgio, please … oh, please…'

Make it worth while, make it something that counts, something that happened to both of us, not just to me.

'Please, what?'

'Can we go to the mountains?'

'But we are going to the mountains. You know that very well. We are on the way. Another two days and we shall be in the Rockies. Now come and find a bar.'

'Promise you won't chase the tornado?'

There is enough fright around without the natural forces taking a hand. Somebody take my hand. I wish Morgan were here to look after me. He has such strong hands.

'We will do only what you please,' said Giorgio.

The Rockies

On the turnpike between Denver and Boulder I saw the mountains first, slashed and rocky, earning their name. They must have been there earlier, but it had been, briefly, a cloudy afternoon.

Giorgio drove in a black silence, not raising his eyes from the road. There had been no letters for him in the post office in Denver.

'Giorgio ... look!'

'I see.'

'But aren't you excited? After two thousand miles of flat country?'

'Yes ... yes.'

I stood up in the open car and hung on to the windscreen.

'Oh, Giorgio ... do stop ... it's so good to be able to breathe again.'

He didn't seem to hear me, he drove even faster and I sat down to save my hair.

'Why did she not write? What can have happened to her?'

He hit the steering wheel.

'She's probably busy.'

'Busy? How can she be more busy than I am? And I am always writing to her ...

always … every day.'

'Not every day, Giorgio … you haven't posted a letter for a week now.'

'How do you know what I have posted? When I am going to the post office? You are spying on me all the time. Cannot I even buy a stamp without your big eyes reproaching me?'

My big eyes – goodness me, when all I'm doing is trying to slip into the post office unnoticed to buy an air-letter for Morgan myself, and then scrawl it standing up while Giorgio is in the bath. Is that what Giorgio is doing when I am in the bath?

'I expect she's on the road, Giorgio.'

'For four hours? She could write before she left and again when she arrived. She has plenty of time.'

'Time goes quickly when you are happy.'

He shook his head firmly.

'She cannot be happy without me.'

Is Morgan happy without me? He never exaggerates in any way, and if you always speak the absolute truth it is hard to catch the exact moment to mention happiness.

'Morgan is going to the seaside, too.'

'Why? Without children there is no need.'

'He is taking a party of other people's children to Aberdovey. It's a seaside town on an estuary.'

'He would do better to occupy himself with you and give you a child of your own.'

'They will go up into the hills ... some will walk well, some will straggle, fall into bogs and even sit on the path and cry. They will be town children who do not know the country and tear up the flowers and shout at the sheep and leave the farmers' gates open, and Morgan will be talking Welsh with the farmers and encouraging the tired children and seeing to their blisters...'

'Is that a holiday?'

'They will swim too ... not in the dangerous quicksands of the estuary, but out in the open sea where the waves knock them down and keep them warm, and they'll come out into a mild drizzle and the towels will be damp before they start, and they'll be living in tents in the sandhills with nowhere to dry anything, so for ten days all their clothes and shoes will be wet and gritty and the children will prick their feet on clumps of sea-holly and some will be hit by stray golf balls...'

Giorgio looked at me with amazed horror and put his hands over his ears.

'Stop, stop ... you are making *me* sad... Is this any way to live? When *we* are at the sea the rocks are too hot to sit on and the water soft and warm. The children are brown like Indians and swim like seals, and they may only prick their feet on the little black *oursins,* and the town lies round the blue water in a circle of pink and brown, and walking up the hill at midday there is the hot smell of piñon.'

There could be no more to say. He left me to brood hopelessly on national character and climate. Daughter of damp and masochism, how could I change? If there was no time for reading, there was even less for a prolonged psychoanalysis which might ease me gently into sensuality. Prayer seemed equally out of place: 'Please God, make me a good mistress' ... coming after years of silence was not a plea to reach the peacock throne.

Giorgio drove slowly through Boulder, making a detour to take in the university campus. The Italian architecture of nearly all the university buildings interested him.

'They are trying with their tiled roofs to make it like a hill town, Siena ... something like that. It is strange.'

I thought he would stop altogether. It was already evening and the red rocks behind the town glowed in the last sun. But he drove on up into the mountains.

'Why didn't we stop there? It's getting late.'

Who knows what happens up in these wild passes with the rustic tables built for picnics?

'Because I have introductions there,' Giorgio explained. 'Another professor in the university. Tomorrow I will visit with him but

84

first I must place you discreetly.'

'Couldn't I go to the university with you?' I asked foolishly.

'Do not be ridiculous.'

After half an hour's silent driving up a twisting gorge, we came to a small dark lake. A little wooden town lay at the far end. 'Here we stay,' Giorgio announced.

He slowed the car over the stony track of the main street and bumped to a stop in front of a ranch-house which seemed to be a sort of hotel, or at least to have rooms over a bar.

We had a window towards the lake. I leant on the sill and breathed pinewoods and water. The high mountains had disappeared again and left smaller, more friendly hills.

'Oh, Giorgio ... I am so happy.'

'I, too.'

He came and leant over me, looking out.

'Are you *really*, Giorgio?'

'You never let one statement pass. Do not doubt so much.'

'It was only ... in the plains it was so hot and dusty and I felt strange and useless and unreal.'

'Why must you always be useful?'

'I don't know ... puritans, I suppose.'

'But at least now in the hills, though you are still not useful, at least you feel real?'

'It is more like home.'

'But *your* green hills are all wet.'

'Not always ... the summer before we married was very hot ... Morgan and I used to lie on the hillside above the town, and it was brown and slippery and no grass left for us to pull and chew.'

'It must be very unhealthy to chew grass like an animal.'

'Don't you have grass in Italy?'

'We have no need to eat it...'

'I thought they were all starving in the south?'

'But in any case there is no grass in the south. Let us not think about starving people. I am starving for you. Come and love me, Rose.'

'Before supper?'

'There are no rules ... love does not respect mealtimes. Kiss me quickly ... hold me.'

'But, Giorgio...'

'You see ... you see how it is. I am angry with myself, but it is all the time like this with you.'

'I thought you were not thinking about me at all?'

'You should try to understand.'

'I do ... I try all the time.'

I listen to every word you say, I watch every passing shadow on your changing face.

'Then do not try so hard ... stop thinking and enjoy yourself.'

'Oh, yes ... if only there were no days –

only nights … cool nights.'

'Cool nights are good.'

'Tonight we shall need blankets … how wonderful.'

He pulled me down with him on the bed.

'Think about me, Rose … not about blankets … cease to be a housewife. You are always so prosaic … I will cover you better than any blanket. Have you no romance in your ordered spirit?'

Those big brown wistful eyes to drown in, one step, two steps out of my depth, floating in my lake, stirring the deep fast currents, moving with all the lilies, all the fishes over the long long falling edge through the rocks and the thunder into the shattered calm which should go on for ever and ever slowly trailing the last lily into a watery grave.

And then when I am dying of learnt love there's Giorgio leaping out leaping up saying:

'Now I am hungry … now, now come along, Rose, quick! I must have a very big steak.'

'Oh, darling—'

'What is the matter with you? You look more beautiful. Get up at once and come down and show the world how beautiful you look because of me, so that everyone will say, "Isn't that woman lucky to travel with an Italian!"'

He roared into the shower, making a great

draught as he passed me on the bed naked and still weak from my brush with eternity.

I rolled over on my stomach to keep the warmth of him from leaving me altogether, and lay there laughing as he started to bellow, 'I am convalescing' from *Traviata* in a fruity tenor.

'Don't go away today ... please,' I said next morning.

I turned in very close to him. He was lying on his stomach now. He put his arm across me, but did not open his eyes.

'It is polite I should go.'

'But this professor never even heard of you ... he does not know you are in the world, let alone you are anywhere near Boulder.'

'He will guess.'

'How can he possibly guess?'

'I wrote and told him I was coming.'

'Oh, Giorgio...'

'*Now* what is the matter?... We must meet Americans ... we are here for that ... why are you always reproaching me? You should be interested in my work, my friends, the colleagues I must meet. International Law is after all an international subject – so why?'

'Nothing ... only...'

'Only what?'

I sat up, pushing my hands into my hair.

'Don't you see ... it's another place I could have told Morgan about if you knew all along you were coming here, it's an address I could have used. I could have got a letter. I haven't had a letter for nearly three weeks now.'

'I do not want you to tell Morgan anything. I don't like this barbarous Morgan.'

'Everyone likes Morgan.'

'Except me.'

'And why should you be so set against him, when you never even met him, I'd like to know?'

'It is obvious.'

'It is *not* obvious. Nothing about you is obvious. I never even know when you are going to clean your teeth.'

'What does it matter when I clean my teeth?'

'I don't mean it *matters* – I only mean I don't know when you are going to do anything like get angry or get up or go to sleep. You don't seem to have any habits ... you are so sudden ... nothing is obvious.'

'And why are you so angry early in the day?'

'Because I don't see why you should hate my husband. It's just irrational and churlish.'

'He should take more interest in you and less in politics.'

'But I believe he is right, individuals are not that important.'

'Rose ... how can you say such uncivilized

things? From that comes the extermination of the Jews.'

I beat on the pillow for want of somewhere to stamp.

'Don't twist me around, you know I don't mean that ... I mean *all* individuals are important ... not just one, not just particularly one woman. I would think less of him if he devoted his whole life to me. What would he do, for heaven's sake? He must work and he is a natural fighter ... and I don't mean with guns.'

'He should believe you exist. A woman cannot exist till she is believed in. I am creating you.'

Smug ... with his eyes still shut. This is not *me,* enraged, in these strange raw mountains. I could see the lake and a little wind went down it shivering the water. I pulled the sheet up to my neck and shivered in sympathy.

'Lie down and listen,' Giorgio said. 'You are making it draughty for me. My father was only interested in politics. He was also a great atheist of his day. Do you know what this means in Italy, in a country where the Church is the supreme ruler of everything? As children, no one would speak to us ... not even the other children at school. If we did not go to Mass we were outcasts from the community and half the time of my youth my father was in prison, my poor mother ... and as soon as I and my brothers got old enough then we too began to go to prison. I remember her always in tears.'

'It is not like that in Britain.'

'You have no children.'

'That has nothing to do with Morgan's politics. I told you why. Anyway, do you listen ... don't change the subject whenever I try to ask you anything.'

'Why don't you get me my fruit juice? There is a habit for you to count on ... without it I am never awake.'

'Giorgio, I mean it.'

I stroked his soft furry chest.

'Please stay here today ... in this lovely place, so that we could have something special to remember – to tell our grandchildren. I don't suppose you can tell your children ... it would be too near. We could take a picnic into the woods. Please. It's the first time we've been anywhere nice together.'

'How can you say that? Was it not nice every time we are loving each other?'

'Yes ... no ... yes, mostly. But don't you see, here it's *every*thing. Good in bed and good outside. It's because of being cool again and the water and the woods. Perhaps we could even make love in the woods?'

'At my age? What a horrible idea!... We should be bitten by wild animals.'

'You think a great bear would come up and take you for a cousin?'

'No … no … ants, mosquitoes … it is dangerous to take off your clothes in any woods… But perhaps there are bears also? I would like to meet a bear. My son would be very pleased for that.'

'Then you *will* stay with me, and we'll go and look for a bear?'

For answer he rolled out of bed and began to dress.

'No … I am going to visit the professor, who is a great friend of mine. But I will stay only one hour, so you may prepare your picnic, and when I return we will go out into the woods and eat it. Perhaps we should go on horses? There are horses here to rent. Then we need not sit on the ground and the horses can fight the bears for us.'

'I can't ride,' I said sadly. 'Or ski.'

'Neither can I,' Giorgio admitted. 'But I think we are not too old to learn, to become like the splendid people. When we are in Colorado we should do what the Coloradans do.'

'But they've been doing it such a long time. They've been splendid people since they were children. I'm frightened of the actual horse, not only of falling off. It's not so much that it's high as it has such big teeth.'

'I also find the appearance of the animal ferocious.'

'How can you say that, Giorgio … and you a man?'

'I am an Italian man. We do not have to pretend to be brave like the British. We are too civilised. Everyone knows that all Italians are cowards. We are always running away. It is our nature. Even from horses.'

He leant forward and peered into the glass.

'I am worried for my face, Rose.'

'What is the matter with your face? I like it.'

'It is beginning to look forty ... you can see here where it is flabby and too yellow.'

'But you are forty.'

'There is no need to give in to this. You should help me to feel young. At heart I am a young man. A very young man. I have not got time to be forty.'

'If you don't *feel* forty it's all right. Anyway you are still extremely handsome, as you well know.'

'My stomach also is spreading.'

He patted it gently and then looked at himself sideways with his jacket buttoned up.

'How do I seem? Very fat?'

'Not *very* fat.'

'How much do you love me?'

'As much as you love me.'

'Not more? You should love me more. You should tell me I am good-looking, young and slim...'

'But only the first one is true.'

'Never mind the truth ... you should say it all the same.'

'Do you always tell all your women they are beautiful?'

'I never tell my wife. Even when she looks very lovely I never tell her.'

'But why ever not?'

'She would become too pleased with herself. What do you say?'

'I say that's very unfair.'

'Always this cricket yearning for fairness. Between men and women there is no such thing. I am now dressed and I still have no fruit juice. Where is it?'

I picked up the telephone.

He started downhill towards Boulder at ten o'clock. From the window I watched him drive away and then went back to bed.

I lay there thinking about holidays ... all my life has been divided into school terms and school holidays. I went from school to college and teaching-college and back to school again as a teacher, and on to the university as a lecturer. Morgan's holidays don't always coincide with mine, but I do external examining and teaching at summer schools, so I don't often have time on my hands. When we are both free together Morgan likes to go walking in the Snowdon district, or the Gower peninsula, or down in Pembrokeshire.

'We have the finest countryside in the

world,' he said once.

Morgan hasn't travelled much, and he doesn't want to either. 'We'll get things right here first,' he says. And he will, too.

So was this a holiday, this spare time I had now with Giorgio? This agonizing struggle to make contact with another human being … could it possibly go under the heading of pleasure? What do the papers mean when they say a pair of lovers are just 'close friends'? How do they manage it? I had now been two weeks entirely alone with Giorgio and I felt further away from him than anyone else on earth. Wearing my eyes out on him told me nothing. I knew the shape of his nose and the size of his mouth and the length of his legs and the width of his stomach and the depth of his eyes … but nothing, nothing of his mind, not what he was thinking, hoping, fearing, feeling at any time. Are there any short cuts? Without going back to live a long hot childhood in Rome, without sharing the palazzos, the prisons, the no-god in a God-shadowed country?

How do the Americans work it out so well in less than a generation, understand and love each other, coming in the middle of the story with only the future in common?

What is the matter with us Europeans?

By two o'clock I felt more European than ever. I ate my picnic alone sitting on a gate staring at horses shining in the sun.

At eight o'clock Giorgio returned in the dark, full of Martinis and good spirits.

'Very interesting people, Rose. The professor will visit with me next year in Rome ... also there were a philosopher, a sociologist ... many more gathered to meet me for lunch and again later on. You would have enjoyed it. Why did you not come?'

In the graveyard in Central City, Colorado, there is a tombstone which reads 'Williams, murdered' and then the date. There were many Welshmen lying up there in the wind and the trees among the other gold-miners. Welshmen who helped to build the little opera house with the big gilt mirrors and keep the alien valleys singing.

'Look, Giorgio ... a Williams ... perhaps he was Morgan's cousin.'

'You should not have let him come.'

'They went farther than that for the gold when it went underground.'

'And what for? To get murdered.'

'Do you think Americans ever die?'

'Why not?'

'We have seen and heard nothing of death till now ... no gardens of remembrance, no funeral processions ... no black hats. These are all old deaths.'

'I heard many sirens in New York. Each one sounds for a death.'

Giorgio drooped against a life-size hacked-out stone tree. On it was written:

'Here lies a woodsman of the world.'

Giorgio's thick plump throat looked very brown now against his white open shirt.

'How do you die in Italy?' I asked him.

'In company. It is sad to die without friends, at that time they are needed more than any other. We all go, friends, cousins, aunts, uncles – and sit with the dying.'

'In the sick room?'

'Why not? If the dying are sick...'

'Don't you use up all the fresh air?'

'Friends are more necessary than fresh air.'

'I think we are more like the Americans, ashamed to die. It is something to do quietly, alone ... an insult to the living.'

'But life is so good because of death. I shall die young.'

'But, Giorgio ... you are already not young, you said.'

'I am at least much too young to die. You admit that, I hope?'

He glared at me.

'And also I know that I am quite ill.'

'You imagine things.'

'No ... I feel it. But I do not regret.'

He began to walk on up the hill towards the thicker pine-woods. As so often, I found myself running after him.

'I wish you didn't walk so fast.'

'I am thinking.'

He had his hands clasped behind his back. 'You should not talk to me of death, Rose.'

'I'm sorry. It seemed natural in a grave-yard, even if we were only there as tourists.'

'It is natural, but I am not ready to die yet.'

'You won't, Giorgio ... you couldn't. You are so much alive.'

'Perhaps ... sometimes. I want to write a book that is not a textbook. I need time.'

'You'll be like that Sicilian prince ... live a long busy life and make a masterpiece in the last six months.'

'I don't like that ... I want to enjoy the life of a genius also.'

He held out his hand ... but not to help me over the stones. He wanted a human being near him, any human being.

'Stay near me, Rose. You are so strong. So healthy. I admire your health so much.'

I laughed. 'Health isn't catching, I'm afraid. It won't rub off on you.'

'Why not? Always making rules for what can happen. Anything can happen at any time.'

He put his arm round my shoulders and leant on me suddenly with all his weight. I stumbled and this time he laughed.

'Perhaps you are not so strong as I think.'

'No, I'm not,' I said crossly, rubbing my ankle. 'Every time I am kind to you, you hurt me. You should ask yourself why you

98

are a sadist.'

Reproach seeped into the big brown eyes again.

'Rose, you should not say such things. I only want to test your kindness.'

'Oh, that's what it is, is it? A test?'

That's one thing I really thought I'd grown out of. I may be a retarded adolescent in the woman of the world department from Giorgio's point of view, but surely, the days of exams are gone for good?

I sat down by the side of the road and took off my shoe to shake out a stone. Giorgio stood in front of me waiting.

'You have very pretty ankles.'

'One of them will soon be very swollen.'

'Poor thing ... poor little thing. Give it to me.'

He took my foot in his hands and rubbed it gently, then bent down and kissed it. No one ever kissed my foot before. It felt very odd. As far as Morgan is concerned I have no feet. I might as well be propelled on wheels for all he knows. Every day with Giorgio I discovered new territories of flesh and bone. Is that so wrong? Twenty years a woman lives with her body ... maybe twenty-five ... not long. There are fifty other years in the mortal span to use for the mind and the memory. I was already half-way along the best time and only now to know that I had feet. I began to laugh again.

'Why are you always laughing at me?' Giorgio asked.

'I'm not. It's my feet.'

'Your feet are not funny.'

'No. The point is I didn't know they were anything.'

'What are you saying?'

'Oh, never mind ... it's too difficult to explain.'

'There is nothing to explain. I understand. It is you who are slow. I told you I would create you.'

I glanced up at him and stopped laughing.

'Don't look at me like that, Giorgio.'

'But I want you.'

My hair was slipping and I pushed it back.

'We were going for a walk.'

'I do not like walking any more.'

'We can go back soon to the hotel.'

'I want you *now* ... not soon.'

Everything was always Now. Now hunger, now thirst, now cold, now terror, now love. My hair dropped heavily into my neck and I pulled out the pins slowly. I had nowhere to put them. Giorgio slipped them into his pocket.

'Come.' He jerked me to my feet and turned into the woods among the flowers ... delicate columbines, wild lupins all shades of purple through to white, something very blue, I'd never seen before, and yellow tansies. I walked carefully, but it was hard not

100

to step on them.

'I thought you said you were too old for love out of doors?'

'Then I was too old. Now I am young again, the flowers make me young. When I was a boy I took my first love up the mountain behind Stresa. First you must ride in a tram up this high hill through chestnut trees for a long while. Then at the top you come to a small albergo where you may eat under the trees ... looking down many thousands of feet to the Lago Maggiore, after that you climb again on foot and go on over the other side down to the woods and the flowers. And there I loved her very well.'

'What was her name?'

'I forget.'

'Oh, Giorgio ... your first love and you forget?'

'Maybe it was not altogether my first. It is a pity there is no grass in these rocky mountains.'

All the lovely flowers were growing out of little stones.

'It will be very sharp for me,' I said nervously.

'Do not think of it ... I will choose you a splendid carpet of flowers, and if you feel anything through that you will be very ungrateful. You will lie there enamelled in jewel colours like a Persian miniature.'

'Persian miniatures aren't enamelled ...

they only seem to be.'

'So you will only seem to be lying in a picture.'

'Yes – really it'll be more like an Indian bed of nails.'

'Do not grumble. You are a very lucky girl. It is not every housewife finds herself in such an interesting position on the top of a very high mountain.'

'I don't think any housewife would envy me this gravel.'

'Do not forget that through the bed of nails the mystic attains the white light of Nirvana. It will be the same for you.'

'Do you think we shall be arrested? I'm sure it must be illegal in the state of Colorado.'

'No, no. They are a good healthy outdoor people with fine mountain scenery. They will not wish to prevent us from having a full enjoyment of their scenery. Besides, Rose, you are making very silly objections. No one can see us here.'

The pine trees were not all that thick, nor the flowers so very tall. I sat down and the columbine tickled my chin.

'What about that woodsman of the world you were leaning on?' I asked, looking round for gamekeepers or possibly bear keepers.

'Excuse me? I was leaning on you.'

'Earlier … in the graveyard … his grandson might slip down a tree any minute with his axe.'

'Please.' He put his arms round me. 'Do not mention the graveyard. I told you I am not ready to think of death. Later. When I am depressed.'

He unbuttoned my blouse and began to kiss me and the purple lupins shimmered and swam together for the last housewife left on earth. I closed my eyes against the afternoon. He drew off my skirt and laid it underneath me.

'There ... the stones will be soft.'

The pink bell of the columbine hung over me now, dipping a little, but the wind was warm.

I had never lain naked in the sun before.

'*Ciao* darling.'

'You are the sun, Giorgio.'

'I am warming you ... you feel me?'

'Yes ... oh, yes.'

'Do not move. Lie still in the sun, loving me.'

'You and the sun.'

They were in my bones together like honey.

New Mexico

'The pleasantest part of a man's life is generally that which passes in courtship, provided his passion be sincere, and the party beloved kind with discretion.'
ADDISON.

Afternoon

When I saw Eagle Nest Lake on the road from Raton I wanted to stop even though it was only early afternoon. Giorgio had planned to push on at least as far as Taos.

'Oh, please, Giorgio, it's beautiful here. Almost like Wales – with those blue and green hills.'

'Cannot anything be beautiful for you unless it is familiar? I find strangeness more interesting.'

But he was in a generous mood and he pulled the car into the motel, a collection of white wooden bathing huts round a gravel courtyard. He swerved to avoid a clump of purple iris growing among the stones.

Later when we went swimming the lake water was iris-coloured and not very warm. Giorgio hesitated on the edge.

'Come on in,' I called.

'It will make me ill.'

'Very refreshing ... do you good.'

'I am not accustomed.'

I turned my back on him and swam away towards a raft. I heard him coming after me ... fast. He caught me up, put his arms round my neck and pulled me down under water. I didn't dare kick him again so I went limp without a struggle, and he let me go. He pushed past me to reach the steps of the raft first, and when I surfaced choking and shook the water out of my eyes, I saw him leaning against the raft laughing at me.

'You look so stupid drowning,' he said. 'So stupid.'

'So would you. It's very difficult to be dignified and drown.'

'But you would try, Rose, wouldn't you? You would keep a stiff upper lip till all the water went up your nose for ever.'

'All your ideas about Britain are so out of date. I'm sure you think everyone there goes about in bowler hats. You should come there and find out.'

'No, thank you. Leave me my dreams ... I see them all in top hats actually, it is prettier.'

I tried to climb up the raft past him but he blocked my way. He slipped down into the water, slid his legs round me and drew me towards him.

'Have you ever made love under water, Rose?'

'No...'

'It is very beautiful ... in the deep rock pools near Portofino...'

'Please let me go...'

'So many things have never happened to you ... I am so sad for you.'

'It's much too cold at home.'

'It is cold here ... but I can warm you very quickly. We can swim together like one whale ... that is why they speak of a whale of a time, I expect, don't you think, Rose? Listen how idiomatic is becoming my English.'

'It's awful ... it gets worse every day. You'd much better start teaching me Italian.'

I tried to push his arms down. His wet hair was flat to his head and his Roman nose looked bigger than ever. Standing on water our eyes were level. He splashed me.

'What do you say? Beautiful stupid drowning Rose?'

'Don't...'

'You like that?'

'You know I do.'

'Tell me you like to feel me everywhere in the water all around you.'

'Let's get out and lie in the sun for a while.'

'I can't get out like this,' he protested. 'You know I can't.'

I wriggled away from him, and managed to drag myself safely up on to the raft. I rolled over well into the middle and lay with my face towards the water. Giorgio swam round and round the raft like a porpoise, complaining.

'You are very cruel.'

'You tried to drown me.'

'I was only trying to love you.'

'Funny way of loving.'

'Not funny at all ... very plain and straightforward. Italian girls especially like that – under water.'

'Do they?'

'An Italian girl would never leave me alone like this to be so ridiculous.'

'But you are only ridiculous under water.'

'I feel bad.'

'But no one can see you ... and pain will widen your grasp of the universe ... anyway, I'm sorry.'

'You are not sorry.'

'Yes, I am. I'm sorry I am so respectable.'

'You are not thinking of respectable ... you are only glad to have me in your power.'

'I don't think in terms of power.'

'How much longer do you think I can keep swimming around like this?'

'It'll be interesting to find out, won't it? They keep people in tanks of water for days in the name of science. I'll take notes.'

I rashly closed my eyes under the hot sun.

I would become a really rich Italian brown all over, a slinky silky nut colour irresistible to Giorgio.

Suddenly the raft tilted under me, Giorgio seized my shoulders and pulled me down into the water on top of him, head first.

We came up fighting. I no longer cared if I hurt his precious liver. I lashed out at him and the water in a welter of futile splashing.

'Let go, Giorgio ... don't!'

'Take me.'

'No ... there are people.'

'Not under water ... as you say. They are far away in a little boat.'

'They are coming nearer.'

'They have their own lives.'

'No ... no ... later.'

'Yes, *now,* keep still ... you are floating ... the water is kissing you ... the water will keep you safe.'

'But I've always been afraid of drowning – it's dreadful.'

'Do not be afraid ... drown with me ... we go down into the dark together. Come ... come now...'

In the middle of the night there was screaming ... somewhere very close. It went on and on. I sat up in the dark and listened. A woman was yelling:

'We aren't happy here ... you bring me all this way...'

I couldn't hear what the man said, his voice was low and grumbling.

'Do something,' she yelled again. 'Do something to make me happy.'

He hit her. I could hear the slap clearly, then she must have fallen against a chair. The crash woke Giorgio.

'They are coming for me,' he said. Calmly nonsensical. He got out of bed bumping in the dark.

'It is time. The fascists are here at last.'

I turned on the bedside lamp, and he stood there in the middle of the room blinking and naked, wondering who I was.

'Giorgio ... it's all right ... wake up ... Giorgio, this is America.'

Next door the woman started to howl very loudly 'boo hoo' like a child.

'It is not right.' Giorgio pulled on his shirt and trousers and started towards the sound. 'Something is the matter.'

'You should not interfere between a husband and wife,' I told him.

'How do you know they are husband and wife? Perhaps they are only like us.'

'And how would you feel if a man came in to interfere between us?'

'There is no need. We have no quarrel.'

There was another loud noise from next door, this time a sort of splintering crack, as if a chair was being beaten to pieces against the wall. Perhaps the woman was against the wall, too.

'Giorgio ... you know you said pain was part of life.'

'Do not be idiotic.'

'And you know you don't like violence...'

'Just because you are afraid to make a scene.'

'It's not that ... only you'll get hurt and it won't do any good.'

But Giorgio had gone. At the same moment a car started up with a jarring grind I'd never heard before in America and roared out of the motel courtyard in a scatter of pebbles.

There were angry voices all round now because the woman was out on her front porch screaming:

'Don't go, Ted ... don't go, Ted ... Ted...'

I went to the window and saw her in a little frilly shortie nightdress in the moonlight beating on the open door. Giorgio put his arm round her shoulders, loosened her hand from the door-knob and drew her inside. Everything grew quiet again. The other inhabitants took their heads in and stopped shouting at her. I thought I heard an owl, or maybe it was a nesting eagle. I put on my own nightdress and got back into bed and lay there with my eyes wide open to the moon squares on the ceiling and my ears stiff with listening.

At first she sobbed ... low and desperate

... then she talked. Giorgio hardly said anything. He would be stroking her hair, sitting on the bed with her head on his knee. Then after a while there was no noise at all, even when I got out of bed and put my ear to the wall. Perhaps she was asleep and Giorgio sitting there afraid to move for fear of waking her. Perhaps he was lying beside her already.

He came back with the light. I shut my eyes and heard him creeping round the room. He edged into bed and lay on the far side without touching me. I will not say anything, I will not. He is free to do as he likes when he likes where he likes. He has promised me nothing. No human being belongs to any other human being, not in the West anyway. So the words came out from the top of my silly head:

'Why were you so long?'

'I thought you were asleep, Rose.'

'No.'

'You should be.'

'I couldn't sleep till you came back.'

'That was foolish. It is good for you to sleep well. It is necessary for your skin now you are not so young.'

'What were you doing?'

I heard the hard edge on my voice. I lay somewhere near the ceiling watching myself. I hate me, Giorgio will hate me too. What a horrible nagging wife woman I turned out to be. And I'm never like this with Morgan either. Stop me talking, Giorgio ... kiss me, love me, tell me I'm alive.

'You've been in there with her two hours.'

'She was very unhappy.'

'But you don't know her.'

'Poor woman ... you should pity her. She is married to a brute.'

'She's a stranger.'

'We should all help each other.'

'Particularly pretty women in very short nightdresses.'

'Rose ... Rose ... Rose... That is not like you. That is a very small way to talk.'

'I feel small ... anyway, you mean mean.'

'How can I mean mean? It is not sense... Is that really how you say it?'

He rolled over towards me, so interested in grammar, and my tears spilled out on to the comfort of his chest. He stroked my hair back from my eyes and waited without saying anything. In the middle of the hot damp relief of crying I remembered that he had just come from another crying woman. One woman in tears might have slight appeal, but two in one night must be too much. I swallowed frantically, rubbing my eyes.

'I'm sorry, Giorgio ... I didn't mean that... It was only I'd been lying awake thinking for so long and she didn't seem to be talking, so I thought ... well, I didn't exactly *think* ... but I felt you'd gone. It's like losing ... I mean it hurts when you go. It's a sort of ache, it's not so much that I mind you being somewhere else, but I mind all over that you aren't here with your arms round me like this. It's become the only way to live with the day not counting at all and I just grudged two hours out of one of our nights because there can't be so very many, can there? Not more than perhaps thirty or forty altogether, do you think? Forty nights in the wilderness?'

He answered me with a heavy snore. His arm round me slackened and fell away. I was alone again.

I got out of bed and sat by the window writing to Morgan in the rising sun.

Morning

I had dressed and started to do my nails when Giorgio woke up.

'I hate that stuff,' he said with his eyes shut still. 'It makes an 'orrible smell.'

'But you like women to be neatly finished off?'

'But by magic ... you should do it in the bathroom, far away from me.'

'I thought you were far away ... asleep.'

'My wife has the maid do her nails for her.'

'Giorgio ... what century are you living in back there in Italy?'

'She likes to do it ... the maid. It is more amusing than polishing the floor. Marble is very hard for kneeling.'

'I never in my life had anyone to polish a floor for me. Even if we had the money Morgan would not allow that.'

'But in Italy the girls *like* to work. It makes them happy. My brother the communist also has three maids. If you live in a capitalist system you must make the most employment possible. It is my duty to make work.'

'I don't think Morgan would approve of it. Why can't you organize workers to reclaim the land in the south and re-house the people?'

'That husband of yours is more stupid everything I hear of him. Life is not so simple as he thinks. He has made your hands like sawdust. For what?'

I looked at my hands surprised. Since I had done no washing up for six weeks they seemed smooth to me. I rubbed my cheek tentatively.

'In any case,' Giorgio raised himself on one elbow, 'where is my fruit juice?'

I walked across to the café and on the way back I saw the girl from next door. She was sitting outside her cabin on her case with a basket beside her. She looked even younger in the sunlight ... not much more than twenty with moony fair hair. She had rather a moony face too, round and pale. She smiled, very friendly.

'Your husband was so good to me,' she said.

'I'm glad.'

'Ted just upped and went.'

'I know … I heard.'

'I don't know what I'd have done without your husband.'

'I'm sure someone would have helped you.'

'He's so kind.'

'Kind? Oh, yes…'

'I'm not accustomed to kindness. It isn't in Ted's nature to be kind at all.'

She didn't look worried. She just sat there with her long brown legs stretched out in the sun, scuffing stones between her bare toes.

'I'm so sorry,' I said. My carton of hot coffee was slipping. I began to edge into our doorway.

'About when do you think you'll be ready?' she asked.

'Ready?'

'Ready to go. It's very good of you both to take me along.'

I tried to look as if I knew, as if it were the most normal thing. If we had been married would it have been normal? Of course, but how far? Where to? Would she still be with us in Mexico City? What on earth had Giorgio said to her?

'I'll ask him when.'

I poured Giorgio's grapefruit juice out of the other carton into a tooth-glass and carried it across to the bed. His eyes had shut again. He must have heard me talking to the girl just outside the window. I wondered whether I would pour the grapefruit juice over his innocent, stubbly face. He opened one eye obviously wondering the same thing.

'Why were you so long, Rose?'

'Chatting to your girl friend.'

'What girl friend?'

'The girl next door.'

'Ah ... poor girl.'

'I hear you invited her to go to Mexico with us.'

'Mexico? ... never ... she must have understood quite wrong. I only offered her a lift to her mother's home in Santa Fé.'

'And how far is that?'

'One day from here ... maybe less. It depends how often we stop.'

I packed in silence. There seemed nothing to say except 'I'm not coming'. Love may be a creator, but jealousy is a wicked destroyer. I was disintegrating every minute. Already I knew that my hair was too dark, too long, too lank, while little Miss Moonshine had every advantage, starting and ending with youth. She looked so young and fresh and soft. I felt my knobbly elbows with the sawdust hands Giorgio didn't like. I was spiky inside and out, the only soft thing about me was my throat, pulpy with swallowed tears. I folded Giorgio's clothes with more care than usual. He got out of bed and disappeared into the bathroom.

Well, Rose Williams, you asked for it... Whatever made you think you could get away with it? One look at you, my girl, you never were and never will be a *femme fatale*. Brush your hair and wrench the comb cruelly through it ... no more dark rivers of night for you. Twist it up tight tight on the top of your head so that the pins hurt and the skin hurts strained back from your ears ... button into a dark dress tight up to that hurting throat. Remember you are basically a teacher, one who knows everything, one who tells the others what to do.

I went over to the window and called out to the girl:

'He won't be long now.'

She turned her head and smiled.

'Thanks ... I'm Patsy.'

'My name's Rose.'

'Hi, Rose.'

'Hullo, Patsy.'

'What part are you two from? The East? You talk kinda funny.'

'Further east than that ... Europe.'

'You don't say ... I'd love to go there.'

Oh, so would I, this very minute. She had drawn a bird in the dust beside her with

118

long wild wings.

'Is that a bird?' I asked stupidly.

She looked at it again.

'Yep ... I guess so.'

'What kind of bird?'

'Any kinda bird ... a flying kind. You interested in birds?'

'No ... not really.'

'Neither am I. Maybe I drew a plane.'

If there were an airfield at Santa Fé and I lay down in front of a plane would they take pity on my no ticket, no money?

Please, Mr Pilot, America is too much for me, too wide, too high, too cruel ... let me out of here, let me out! I want to be with Morgan in those damp sand dunes splintered with sea-holly, this sharp sun is too hard. Too hard on my creased neck.

Pasty sat full in it with nothing to protect her head. If her world had really fallen round her ears she seemed contented out there in the warm ruins. Contented to wait for Giorgio.

Giorgio came out of the bathroom very spruce, a silk scarf round his neck and a fresh white sports shirt loose over his Who's-for-Tennis linen slacks. I nearly laughed when I saw how hard he was holding in his waist-line. He put his cheek to mine so that I could feel the smoothness and smell the cologne.

'Very nice,' I said gently.

'Kiss me, Rose.'

'Why? To wish you luck?'

'What luck?'

'Never mind.' I kissed him on the cheek. I began to hope that Patsy would appreciate his efforts.

'I go to help the poor girl with her things.'

I waited for him to take ours out with him, but he went out humming and empty-handed, so I collected his shaving lotion from the bathroom, banged it in on top of the silk shirts. After I had got the case shut with a struggle, I saw his brushes out by the bed. I nearly left them, but I've never liked to waste things and they were pretty brushes with G in silver on the back, so I put them into my case and staggered out kicking the doorstep and the side of the car. Giorgio was crouched down beside the girl, he jumped up and bounded to my side lithe as a practising tiger when he saw me.

'Rose … you should not do that,' all affectionate consternation. 'I was just coming back.'

'You were?'

'Of course.'

He stowed everything away.

I guessed I would ride in the back today with the girl in front, but I guessed wrong. Giorgio decided it would be more fun to have us both in front, the girl in the middle, next to him, close to him, pushed up against him … while I edged out towards the knobs on the door.

'This is real nice of you.'

Patsy beamed at me as we swung down the side of the lake.

'Am I going to surprise Ted!' she added.

'I thought you were going to your mother?'

'My mother lives right over in Buffalo.'

I looked at Giorgio, but he did not seem to be listening. He is always acting up like a deaf person when other people are talking English. Half the time he seems not to understand a word and then suddenly he says something and he was following all along:

'What do you say?' He broke in: 'Shall we visit Taos?'

'I thought we *had* to visit Taos?'

'Visit well – study the Indian fashion of living…'

'Patsy is in a hurry to get back to her home … aren't you, Patsy?'

'No hurry at all. Don't mind me. Taos is very interesting. You should stop there awhile. All the tourists in the area go to Taos. And Los Alamos.'

Perhaps a tourist is what I am, that gives me a definition, a character to live in. But where is my camera? So that the future can be more real than the present, the coloured slide brighter than the live morning, because how can anyone trust their eyes to take home an old moment? My eyes could see Giorgio peering ahead at the white road in his dark glasses, but Patsy was heavy against him all down one side. I could only feel that warmth filling the car, I could not see it.

Oh, try try to understand what it is like to be a man, to enjoy a delicious young girl like a slice of chocolate cake as soon forgotten, sex without love, bodies without meaning. I nearly groaned out loud with the physical pain of it, while half of me still argued reasonably, seeing all sides as usual of the question. What question, any question … Giorgio's side, the sensible side. You came with your eyes open, there is no future in this, you are only a tourist, naturally Giorgio is taking this fine opportunity to know an average American better. Then why, oh why, doesn't he talk to her? Why this sleepy humming silence, her eyes drooping, his hand not steady on the wheel? Why are my breasts aching for the slight touch of that particular unsteady hand? Nothing reasonable about those strong brown not even elegant rather stumpy fingers. Perhaps I could fling myself across her into his lap, send the car spinning down the hillside, screaming for help.

Giorgio – you let me out of this iron lung … these hard bones that hold me, don't lock me in again now so soon … don't go, Giorgio, don't go. He would only look coldly at me, his arm round Patsy, and call me stupid. His lips in Patsy's hair he'd call me impatient. His wife, he never tires of saying, has so much patience with him ... well, and so what would this patient wife do now, I wonder? She would smile, be gay, the life of the party, talk all the time, limpid Italian phrases, make the girl her best friend. My throat was still so thick with tears I dared not speak at all. I tried to look out at the narrow wooded canyon, to wonder about the lives of the people in the few houses round the gas station, to be an intelligent tourist and burst out of the cocoon of Giorgio, which obscured the landscape of the United States, but I had no mind left, no guiding sense to steer me through this misery. Everything was reduced to an aching effort to keep the hurt hidden, to hold the tears steady in my rigid head.

Patsy offered us both some gum. I refused, but Giorgio took a piece. Now they both sat, their mouths moving round sympathetically in unison. I began to laugh softly, then wildly till the tears came and I could pretend they were tears of laughter.

'Rose ... what is so funny now?'

Giorgio's hurt voice.

'I'm sorry ... oh dear ... it was the gum, trying to be an American you look so silly.'

I said it in French.

'I am not trying to be an American. I often chew gum at home. It is very good for the teeth. My children also drink Coca-Cola. Why not?'

'Oh, no reason … no reason at all … you just look funny.'

'You should take good habits of the Americans without scorn, no need to be ashamed.'

He had rebuked me in French and then turned to Patsy to say:

'I'm sorry, that is not polite of us.'

'Go right ahead,' Patsy told him. 'Don't mind me. I majored in French at Albuquerque anyway.'

'You did?'

'Why sure … always wanted to go to France. I don't understand all you said, but I can follow quite a bit…'

So for the next hour Giorgio played happily at being a Frenchman. He tried her out with simple little phrases and more difficult phrases, with a patience he had never shown when trying to teach me Italian. He laughed at her round American way of speaking, but kindly and with pleasure.

'Non, non … pas comme ça … repetez … et encore…'

So she said it again … over and over, giggling sweetly, tossing back her loose hair, a child on holiday from the brutality of the invisible chair-smashing Ted, living in the lovely moment, in the cadences of Giorgio's soft approval. Giorgio's French accent was better than mine, but his knowledge of grammar far from perfect. Several times I had to bite my tongue to prevent myself from interrupting this love duet on a point of syntax.

So I was holding the schoolteacher tight in my rigid heart too, and with despairing pride. I may be no good as a mistress out of school, but back there in safe Wales where I know my students, I can teach. I can teach all right, but I so much wanted the luxury of learning. And he said he would only love the mice women who needed love. Show me the mouse deep down in this voluptuous amiable blonde. Show me why she has to be taught foreign languages and touched by foreign hands.

We reached Taos by lunch-time and after the routine call at the post office ate French food in a dimly lit restaurant at wooden tables.

'Here we stay,' Giorgio announced. 'That is now decided.'

'By whom?'

'By me, of course ... one man, two women ... naturally I decide.'

'Naturally, but what about Patsy? You don't consider her; she must get home tonight.'

'Why?' asked Patsy, her blue eyes alight with wine.

They both turned on me, hostile and together.

125

'Yes, why?' Giorgio echoed her.

I tried to remember why.

'I thought she wanted to surprise Ted … walk in on him just after he gets back.'

'Maybe he didn't go home.' Patsy pushed away her coffee cup and put on fresh lipstick. She could not be the same girl who did all that nocturnal screaming. No scream ever crossed those pearly teeth.

'She cannot go to an empty house. She must allow a little time.'

Giorgio paid the bill and gathered up the change. 'Now that it is all settled we must find a motel.'

He drove us slowly round the little central square of adobe houses – every shop-window glowed with Indian silver and tourist turquoise – and then at random down a side-road out of the town. He chose first a motel in a garden, but it was already full. Across the road was another in the shade of very tall trees. I was pushed to the front this time.

'I have only one double left,' the manageress told me, 'and a single in with another gentleman.'

I looked at Giorgio doubtfully. He was playing his deaf game and staring out of the window with his hands behind his back. I touched his arm and he swung round.

'Giorgio … she says she's only got one double and the single is with another man. Let's go somewhere else. There must be lots

126

of other places ... or we could push straight on to Santa Fé so easily.'

'Why? I want to stay here. I go with the man and you and Patsy together.'

'Oh, *no!*'

'Why not? Why are you so difficult? It is only for one night.'

'Maybe I'd better get the coach from here,' Patsy suggested, but not firmly.

Giorgio strode up to the desk and held out his hand for the keys.

'That will be satisfactory,' he told the woman, and signed the register under all our separate names.

It was the first time my name had appeared since New York. I looked at it in astonishment, hardly recognizing it any more.

I took a long time to unpack one nightdress and longer still to wash. Patsy pulled a comb through her hair, apologized prettily for separating me from my husband, and ran out to join Giorgio in the garden. They walked up and down on the gravel in the shade of the trees. I could hear their laughter, but not what they were saying. Now I was alone I no longer wanted to cry. The tears had hardened. I looked at my face severely, it had grown longer and more sallow, my eyes seemed larger and more sullen. I reminded me of the Charles Addams treewoman in the *New Yorker,* with my dark hair worn like curtains. I glanced at my feet ...

127

no tree roots sprouting, but this would all make a fine story to amuse someone with one day ... Morgan, for instance... How I thought myself beautiful, how I tried so hard to be wicked and sensuous, and how I ended up chaperoning a girl young enough to be one of my own students.

I tightened my hair deliberately, put on my flat sight-seeing shoes and my dark glasses and walked out grimly with my chin up to be responsible Mrs Williams, the reliable guardian of any outing.

Giorgio looked at my feet first and then screwed up his eyes at my hair. But he didn't say anything. He turned on his heel and opened the door of the car. Patsy stood back and I climbed in beside him this time. I could not stop my arm from shaking, so I tried not to touch him.

'Why the disguise?' Giorgio asked in French.

'What disguise?'

'You have put on those terrible shoes again. I told you never.'

'Did you?'

'You do not wish to please me. That at least is clear.'

'We are going sight-seeing.'

'That is no reason to turn yourself into a refugee scarecrow.'

Patsy either didn't understand any of this hissing, or politely pretended not to. She cut across to ask where we were going.

'To see Lawrence's ranch,' Giorgio told her. 'Because it is so interesting to Rose who comes from Britain, and is a scholar some-times. Have you brought your note-book, Rose?'

'And what about the footnotes for the Encyclopaedia of American women?'

He didn't bother to answer that one, so I stared ahead at the grey sage bushes and the withered mesquite clumped against the wires, feeling desert inside and out. But when we turned off the high road into the pine woods and climbed and bumped and climbed six miles up a winding dust-track to reach the house, I gave in to the country after all.

'I never was here before,' Patsy said, get-ting out of the car, just like me and the Tower of London. 'Why, it's so small. Why do they call it a ranch? It belongs to the University of New Mexico.'

She meant the house presumably, the little ordinary locked-up house, but I was looking at the sky, the enormous sky and the wide wide red plain and the blue and purple mountains. I did not know what to do, I could not breathe enough, see enough with the size of my lungs and eyes. I was al-together too small, I needed to be one of a crowd of five thousand from the valleys singing their hearts out as they sang for

129

Nye's death.

'*Che bello,*' Giorgio said quietly, and I turned and smiled at him.

Why could I not say, and really feel, something so simple?

For him it was not trite ... at that moment the beauty of New Mexico possessed him entirely, he wore it all over his face. He smiled back at me.

'You see, Rose? You understand?'

'No ... nothing ... but I don't care any more.'

'All will be well.'

'If you say so.'

'This time it is like home for me ... the piñon smell hot and good.'

'Come and see the quaint little chapel.'

Patsy called back to us. She had gone ahead of us up the path.

I loosened the neck of my tight dress, slipped off my shoes and followed Giorgio with the warm dust between my toes. Quaint was the right word, quainter far to me than any old Tudor Tea Shoppe or spinning wheel. Frieda's large stone tomb guarded the entrance to the shrine with a photograph of Frieda let into the headstone. The chapel looked like an old garden shed, dark-swathed in branches of dying greenery, a tea-chest stacked with ragged sleeping-bags, Lawrence's old typewriter and on the altar a picture of a man in a brown city suit with his arms wide to the rising sun of New Mexico beside the Ashes.

I read the certificate on the wall by which the French mayor guaranteed the Ashes, and studied the enormous visitors' book. A large chunk of the top of the book had been chewed by chipmunks but, as far as I could see, in the last thirty years only about a dozen people had come from Britain, of which four were called Huxley, Auden, Isherwood and Spender.

'Look, Giorgio, so few ... isn't it strange?'

'I am looking...'

'What's the matter?'

I turned round to see him dark and furious.

'Your feet, Rose ... your feet.'

'What is the matter with my feet? I thought you liked them.'

'To walk like that... Put your shoes on at once.'

'I left them in the car.'

'It is madness.'

'Why?'

'How do I know why? Snakes, scorpions, this is a wild country ... poisoned thorns ... everywhere poison ivy.'

I laughed and started to ask Patsy to support my idea of the safeness of New Mexico, but Giorgio had literally swept me off my feet and was carrying me back down the hill.

'Who do you think you are? Rossano Brazzi?' I stopped struggling in his arms ... the whole situation was ridiculous. I smiled, and tried to look happy.

'You are very heavy,' Giorgio panted.

'Then put me down ... for heaven's sake.'

'How do I know what is on this path?'

'Just because your eyes are bad ... I came up it all right.'

'You are behaving like a child ... at your age it is stupid to run barefoot in any country.'

'At your age it is stupid to risk carrying heavy women. You'll get a rupture and anyway what about your liver?'

He groaned and dropped me uncomfortably against the car. We stood glaring at each other and then he took a deep breath and started up again towards Patsy, who was still wandering in the pine trees.

As soon as he turned his back I began to run down the dust-track away from the car, away from Giorgio, into the green silence made noisy only by the noise I carried with me, scattering stones and sobbing. I hate him – hate him ... want to go home, home to a grey silence where no demands are made, where love is easy and gentle and taken for granted with the rain and constant cups of tea. There is no resting place in all this, every minute changes. Just when unified by the gigantic beauties of Nature torn apart again by a silly pair of shoes. What is he doing to me? What does he want? Why look after me with such hatred? Is there no tenderness to spare? But that is all for the family, the patient wife, the splendid children–What did I ever expect? Why did I come with him in the first place? To see America? Have a good time? Certainly neither of these had happened ... they were both too rational. I came because he kissed me ... as simple as that, as any pop song, I forgot everything ... Morgan's decade of trusting affection, Morgan's fight for Wales and Labour and Disarmament, my own students, my pride in my tidy housekeeping, went with Giorgio's quick tongue. Now stop it, Rose ... stop being sorry for yourself, he told you not every ten-years-married wife has a lover at all, let alone Latin, what a fine distinction ... there's lucky you are ... were ... might have been. Kneeling on prickly pine-needles in a foreign forest take heart alone. All Lawrence wanted was for people to be warm-hearted ... men with women ... let's have a try at that. Takes two to make a warm heart, but the effort should be worth while.

I dusted down my dress and started walking with great calmness. The road twisted round the trees and came out farther on, below me. I reached it in a few minutes before I saw the car bouncing down the track. Giorgio was driving far too fast, I could hear his fury in the stones. He skidded and screeched to a stop and then pushed open the back door for me without a word. I got in, in disgrace, and put on my shoes.

'You must forgive her,' Giorgio said to Patsy. 'I'm afraid she is sometimes hysterical.'

'You don't say.' Patsy smiled at me without surprise. 'Do you feel better now, Rose?'

'Yes, thank you … it must have been the heat.'

'Ted's like that. Always going off … I never know if he's gone for an hour or a week … off his head or up the mountains.'

She opened her bag and gave me some paper tissues. When I looked at my face in the driving mirror I saw why … it was streaked grey with dust and tears. I met Giorgio's stony eyes, Italian women never look a mess in public. I licked the Kleenex and went to work on my cheeks without much hope.

Giorgio was giving Patsy some erroneous information about Lawrence.

'He was out in the desert for many years. He was one of those Englishmen who do not really like women.'

'Wrong man,' I snapped, with my mouth full of hairgrips.

'Perhaps he was not so wrong. One begins to understand that. Englishwomen are very hard for anyone to like.'

'You are talking about T.E.'

'The English are always talking about tea.

134

In the desert he must have made it all day.'

'Doubtless using the water stored in the camel humps.'

'Excuse me?'

'Oh, forget it. The English are very fond of animals, too. They'd never dream of draining a hump.'

'We have a lovely dog at home,' Patsy said. 'She's an English sheepdog. She's real gentle with my little girl.'

'Ah, you have a little girl?'

'Sure ... she's eighteen months now.'

'My compliments, madam, and you are so young yourself. You see, Rose, there is nothing to be afraid of. She must be ten years younger than you.'

'You don't have kids?'

'My wife thinks it would spoil her shape. She has a very nice shape, you see.'

Patsy turned round to look at me with kindly interest.

'I never would have guessed you were over thirty ... I was afraid I'd lose my waistline, too. But I've got back to twenty inches now. It took around a year. You should see Suzy, she's a real doll, worth a waist or two.'

'Who is looking after her?'

'Ted's mother right now ... she pinches her off me every minute she can. She's always saying, "Why don't you two go off for a few days on your own, and let me mind Suzy?" She'll be mad at me coming home so soon.'

'You aren't going home yet,' Giorgio told her.

All through dinner he wooed her and she didn't even seem to notice. He asked her about her daily life in minute detail, what time she got up, what she gave the baby for breakfast, when Ted left the house, what she planted in the garden. How had she finished college with Suzy in her arms, what she hoped to do with her life. She did not seem to mind that I was there too, she talked to us as one corporate person. If Giorgio asked all the questions and I only listened, that was because tonight I was a good passive wife encouraging her husband's interests. And my husband is particularly interested in young blondes. Why not? It is a fashionable interest and probably binds the men of the world together better than any ideology. If there were enough jazz, enough football, enough young blondes to go round, would that finish the eagerness to make war? All we dark women, particularly those past thirty, should rise above the personal aspect of this problem.

We were drinking Californian wine. Giorgio pretended to despise it, but he sent for a second bottle very soon. I began to feel detached and benign. Let the young people enjoy themselves, I thought, after all my poor husband is very insecure, very unsure of his attractions, he must prove that paunch is an illusion. Whose husband? Which young people? What blondes? What war?

The third bottle of wine seemed to be with us in the car. Briefly, and by mistake, I was the woman in the middle. Giorgio, looking straight ahead at the road, ran a hand along my thigh.

'Ah – the absent-minded professor.'

'Excuse me?'

'Who was that little attention meant for?'

'Don't be like that. I want you to be happy, Rose, believe me.'

'Oh, yes … what a good idea.'

'But I like everyone around me to be happy. It is so pleasant to see only smiling faces.'

'It must be.'

'Here … stop … turn in here,' Patsy cried, and I found they had brought me to a circle of wooden benches to watch a blazing bonfire and, in a jingle of feathered bells, a troupe of Indians dancing with stamps and flutters for the tourists. I was thankful Morgan was not there, he'd have been appalled at the commercial exploitation and spent the rest of the evening trying to track down the surplus profits and re-distribute them fairly.

Giorgio poured the wine into two cardboard cups. I shared his, but he also drank a little from Patsy's.

'Otherwise you have too much,' he laughed.

'Go right ahead,' she told him.

137

Now he sat between us.

'You see, Rose, those Indians are not entirely corrupted ... that Bird Dance is really very fine.'

'It is cruel to let the little boy dance with toothache.'

'But they say it is their custom. Perhaps he dances better, with more beauty for the pain.'

'There you go ... sentimental about pain again.'

'In any case they probably only say that to impress the tourists.'

'His face looks swollen, poor little thing ... only six years old. Would you let your Janni dance in that state?'

'Janni is not an Indian.'

'A child is a child ... anywhere.'

'I doubt it ... Patsy, do American children dance with toothache?'

But why are they whispering? You don't have to whisper about children and toothache. Has she got toothache? with that round chubby face all pink in the flames, who can tell? Why doesn't she get up and dance, so we can all see how gay and uncorrupt the Youth of America is without a toothache in its head. It's the water. Something in the soil or not in the soil. How many soils in the forty-nine States? How many States in fifty? How many States have I not seen, skimming across the surface of

New York, Pennsylvania, Ohio, Indiana, Missouri, Kansas, Colorado, New Mexico with my eyes on Giorgio? What is the state of Giorgio? How are the mountains and the plains of my love? the rivers and the sands of my love? My love is like a red desert where nothing blooms this June... Ho ho, Giorgio ... I see you pinching her too ... why doesn't she squeak? Perhaps her squeak is broken, the silly sweet doll. Oh, Giorgio, I'm so tired, so sad ... no fun for anyone ... if you pinched me I should only cry. I don't know how to giggle any more. Please take me home. Home got adrift lately, I wanted to make my home in you and I haven't got a toe-hold even, not a rocky ledge to hang on to... Oh, Giorgio, please hear my silent screaming.

'What is the matter, Rose?'

'Nothing.'

'Your eyes are watery.'

'It is the smoke.'

'You are sad.'

'I've got toothache.'

'We will go back in just a short time.'

But it was a long time still. Time in a bar on the main square, time flowing down in whisky. Patsy is drinking blood, she's a jolly little vampire, why doesn't she take scotch like any sensible geisha girl? I'm not used to whisky, but look at me putting it away. Look at me, Giorgio ... look at me. I'm riding without holding on. I'm swimming without any hands. That's not tomato juice, she's fooling you...

'Rose ... are you all right?'

'Why not ... why not all right?'

'We go back now.'

'Don't want to go.'

To be shut up alone with this vampire, beating on the mosquito-wired windows, yelling through the bars for a never coming always far away snoring Giorgio.

'You are time for sleep now,' Giorgio said.

Oh, I am time for you ... you are my timekeeper. Don't put me away.

'Let's go dancing, dear Giorgio dear?'

'No, Rose ... you are not for dancing tonight. And three together is not so good.'

Ah, not so good indeed, not anywhere. I seem to have heard that before, particularly three in a bed you said you didn't like. Who would be in the middle then?

'When the girls came out to play, Giorgio Porgio ran away.'

'You are not right, Rose.'

'I want a drink.'

'You had a drink.'

'I forget them all ... they are all gone into a world of light.'

'Too many drinks.'

'Come along, dear.'

Now old mother Patsy had my other arm and they were both half carrying me through the door. If Morgan could only see me. Would he be surprised? I never was drunk in my life before. Funny funny no feet. I like to be carried about. Somebody's baby. My legs are so tired and my face and my heart.

'She is often like this,' Giorgio sighed. 'I have many difficulties with her.'

'Isn't that just too bad.' Patsy sounded very sympathetic. 'Ted's the same. I can't keep him off it … and he gets so *wild*. He's so big, I can't handle him at all. He's got a real liquor problem. Rose is quiet enough.'

'Do not upset yourself for her. I am sure she will be good in bed. She won't trouble you then. She will sleep in no time at all.'

My head fell on to Giorgio's shoulder in the car and he let it lie there.

'We'll tuck her up and then we might go dancing when she's comfortable,' he suggested.

'Thanks all the same, but it's been a long long day, and I'm short on sleep from last night,' Patsy told him. 'And I don't think she'd be happy on her own.'

'She will sleep, I tell you.'

Through my frozen shut eyes I could feel his frowning. I will not sleep, I tell you, I will not sleep for a hundred years, lying awake waiting for you to kiss me.

'Not tonight, Giorgio,' Patsy still being sweet and polite, 'you've been very good to me.'

To her he is a very old man, a funny old sugar daddy. Let it rest, Giorgio, she doesn't even want you. She hasn't even guessed that deep down you are irresistible. Do you always only want people who don't want you? But if I didn't want you now would you even notice? How do you force someone with their bones full of blondes to look at you not wanting them? Look at me not wanting you, Giorgio, look at me.

'You stay in the car,' Giorgio told Patsy. 'I will put Rose to bed. I won't be long.'

'I'll help you.'

'I can manage her … I am so accustomed.'

But all the same Patsy was competently there on the other side heaving me forward into the bleak white bedroom with the blue beds. Two blue beds. I leant on Giorgio, my eyes more or less shut, and swayed so that he fell against the wall with my weight on him.

'Please wait outside,' Giorgio told her, 'while I get her in. She would be ashamed for you.'

Patsy went out like a good girl. I heard her footsteps on the gravel and the slam of the car door behind her. Giorgio listened too, then he pushed me down and began to wrestle with my clothes. I was no help, no help at all. Shoes fell easily to the floor, but my dress fastened at the back and my bra was all twisted. I twisted too and as his arms

142

went round me for the fastening he lost his balance and fell across me. I opened my eyes very wide.

'*Ciao*, Rose … you are there?'

'Where else?'

'I thought you were passed away.'

'"Passed out" is correct.'

'Always grammar.'

'Only pretending. Very clever.'

'Very naughty.'

'Yes, Giorgio.'

'You make me so much trouble.'

'Yes, Giorgio.'

'I am all the time worrying about you.'

'You should do that. Worry about me. I like it. I flower under it.'

'How is this stupid fastener?'

I showed him.

'I do not like this undressing. It takes too much time.'

'But a lovely delaying time.'

His hands began to move over me with feeling.

'I am very angry with you.'

'Yes, Giorgio.'

'I am going to punish you.'

'Yes.'

'To hurt you.'

But his hands did not hurt, nor the hardness of his mouth.

'It's so light.'

'You do not need the dark, Rose.'

'It hurts my eyes.'

'Then I hurt your eyes. It is your punishment.'

Poor Patsy ... sitting in the car ... alone – unloved.

'Oh, Giorgio ... I thought...'

'Don't think ... I am coming.'

And all the desert of the day flowered into night into light and warmth.

In the morning I knew why Morgan doesn't drink ... why I don't drink. I've never felt so bad, even with jaundice. For a long time I listened to the rasping of Patsy's legs on the sheets, the crash of her bare feet on the floor, the thunder of her low humming as she crept about the room trying so loudly not to disturb me. When I managed to raise my eyelids slightly she pounced at once:

'You sleep right on, dear.'

She tucked the sheets round my chin as if I were her baby.

I struggled up slightly.

'Got to get up.'

'Don't you move ... all the time in the world, Giorgio says. My, that man of yours ... had me danced off my feet last night.'

'Dancing?'

'We found a cute little place with a juke box. They stayed open just for us.'

'Last night?'

How many days and nights had I lain here

in this creaking alcoholic discomfort? Surely last night Giorgio was here, last night, Giorgio was with me and I so much with him. How many Giorgios were there? Some in bed with me? Some out dancing with Patsy? She was brushing out the moonshine fluff round her round face.

'It's so sad you don't like dancing, Rose.'

'Don't *like* it?'

'Giorgio says you never will ... you should, sometime you know.'

'It's not quite like that...'

'Oh, I know one gets tired, but I think it's always worth going out.'

'Oh, so do I.'

'You know, it's the other way round with us. I love it and Ted won't.'

'That's strange.'

'Isn't it? Tell the truth I thought Giorgio would be too old. I hope you don't mind my saying that?'

'Oh, not at all ... not at all.'

'Frankly ... I didn't think he looked that mobile. He's quite a goat in his own way, isn't he?'

'A goat?'

'Oh, I'm sorry ... I shouldn't have said that ... I don't mean *that* way.'

I tried to sit up:

'You want to get back to Ted.'

I fell back groaning, my head stabbed with knives.

'No hurry on my account, I'm having a real good time,' Patsy cooed. 'I promised I'd take Giorgio out to see the Indian village this morning. You lie right there and rest.'

I lay right there.

'I wanted to see the village, too. All those little houses one on top of the other.'

Tears slipped into my eyes.

'Just a collection of old mud huts ... five floors high with Cadillacs at the front doors. Nothing to it, they don't even let you go inside their homes. But we'll bring you back a card.'

'Thanks.'

'Would you like a cup of coffee?'

'No – thanks.'

'Sleep better without.'

And she was gone.

My father always went inside their homes. We'd start out from his dreary office in Cathedral Road in his Morris minor, soon away from the red and yellow brick into the green of the Vale of Glamorgan. We might have been a hundred miles from any coal mines. His work was with the farmers, he was agent for several big estates and there's hours I've spent sitting on gates, picking wild white violets, scratching pigs, while my father paced a field or measured a roof, or stood in silence with the farmer staring at a wood until I thought they must have some secret language. But afterwards it was always:

'Cup of tea, Mr Jones?'

And in we'd go to the warm kitchen with the dark dresser, and the cup of tea turned out to be a big meal of ham and home-made scones and sometimes my father and the farmer and his wife spoke Welsh together. I wish I'd learnt Welsh as a child, I could have been more help later to Morgan, but my father never saw the use of it, he wasn't much of a nationalist. He was proud that I spoke French well, it seemed to him a European language was more use in the world I was growing up into. Morgan was dead against my father at first ... an old reactionary ... a middleman in a wicked capitalist system. Why couldn't the farmers own the land they'd farmed for generations? The issues never seemed as clear as that to me, bribed, as Morgan would say, with home-made scones and violets, 'You never went into the labourers' cottages,' Morgan fierce for the rights of the people, all the people – 'you'd have seen different then ... no ham for tea there ... you came like a damn Lady Bountiful from the smug old middle classes.'

'But, Morgan, I didn't *bring* the ham ... it was there already.'

'You probably ate up all a week's ration for them...'

'I never ... I'm not a pig.'

'Anyway, you vote Labour from now on, Rose Jones, and I'll overlook your murky

147

past … I'll even make you Rose Williams.'

'Kind you are … but remember I don't have a bad past. I never voted yet at all – so you keep your blackmail to yourself.'

I lay and thought about blackmail. Who could write to Morgan and say:

'As a well-wisher, I think you ought to know that your wife is carrying on with an old Iti. Not *that* old either, it seems he's a very fine dancer.'

Morgan would probably write back, if he had an address, a long reasonable letter explaining that his wife was a free agent, that he did not possess her and never had, that marriage was no prison sentence, that if she cared to make a fool of herself in foreign lands that was her affair. Strictly her affair.

No doubt at all he'd be good and sensible and forgiving and take her back with a kindly kiss. So where would the old black-mailer be then? It would be the other way round, of course. The blackmailer would come to me and say: 'I'm going to write to Morgan,' and I would have to explain it was all a waste of time. Poor blackmailer.

A large mosquito on the ceiling had beaten the netted windows … maybe Patsy let it in as a parting present. I lay hopelessly waiting for it to smell human flesh. Several times it zoomed past, missing me, finally it bit me on the eyelid. That's it then, I'm not staying here to be insulted, even by a mangy

148

mosquito. So I sat up again, more firmly, and by degrees, taking whole minutes between each thing, particularly shoes with all that nasty stooping, I put on my clothes and screwed up my hair. With dark glasses I could just bear the sun dashing against the little stones outside. The car had gone all right, no tourism for me. No treats today.

I began to walk along the dusty road towards, for no particular reason, the centre of the town, bumping against the adobe walls. My eye had swollen to add to the unsteadiness of my legs. My head was full of little stones, it needed a good scrubbing out. As a child I was always scrubbing my mother's gravestone in the Cathedral cemetery. Long green stains from the lime trees above, my father didn't like the look of ... taking Vim and muddy water to it, like a slut's doorstep.

'You should bring me down a bucket of hot water from the house,' I told my father.

He looked shifty as he did when faced with any manual labour.

'The stream'll do, Rose, if you scrub hard.'

'You should have ordered granite in the first place if you wanted it gleaming always.'

'Granite's an unfeeling stone.'

'Maybe ... then let this limestone rest. Let it green over.'

'It shouldn't look uncared for. Your Aunt Wyn is coming on Sunday. She'd have something to say.'

I nearly said: 'Break your own knees then over it,' because given my way I'd have grown ivy and dandelions and moss there and let it go all the sooner to damp dust. But he looked so forlorn, my father, liking things nice, but always having to ask someone else to do it, that I hadn't the heart. I scrubbed for him, and then he laid a wreath of roses that Sunday ... my mother's name was Rose, too ... for Aunt Wyn's benefit and my mother's old birthday so long ago. After all, I never knew her, never at all. One baby was the finish of her, poor soul. I took her life and her name as well. Pretty well the finish of my father, too. He did his job all right by me, sent me to Howell's and to college, but I never knew him more than half alive, *partly* interested, *mildly* amused. Maybe he never was more than that in his best days ... but I felt I got the back end of his life and he really went out along with my mother.

There were lumps of turquoise in the little shop and hanks of silver and a sack of amethysts. Is that what they were? Purple living glass ... all shapes – hearts and kidneys.

I stayed in the dark shop a long time ... just because it was blessedly dark ... like someone in a bookshop, reading the stones, running them slowly through my fingers. In the end I bought a turquoise mouse, little and cold and smooth to be company in my pocket. We'll go home, mouse, very soon, home to the soft rain. There is nothing to wait for now. I wish the sun would rain on my hot head in this dry town. My throat is swelling and throbbing like dying of thirst. Maybe I'm getting ill ... very ill of fever or plague. Morgan is so good when I'm ill, patient and strong ... Father and mother he is to me then, and I am a stupid old child with an unused body and an unused face moving through my life sideways – a pink crab too hard outside, too soft inside.

In the drug store I drank the fruit juice standing up to get my arms on to the cold comfort of the counter. How did Giorgio begin the day without me and his fruit juice? I never before in my too long sheltered life had nowhere to go. I went to school, I went home, I went to college, I went home, I went to father, I went to work, I went to Morgan.

It is Tuesday perhaps. Somewhere about Tuesday. It has a Tuesday feel ... yes, the girl says right, it's Tuesday indeed. Sometime late in June by now ... at least we started early in June because in June it's not so hot, and now it *is* so hot. Or don't they call this hot? Perhaps we have finished with June and I never noticed it going with roses and strawberries and too many exams. This is still that test. Giorgio's test. Kind Giorgio is giving me a test. It is all part of a big plan to help me grow up. Giorgio is very kindly helping me to grow up, to suffer, to understand like other women. Like Italian women for instance, who understand everything. What they know instinctively we have laboriously to learn: how to dress, how to love, how to entertain, how to make somebody else cook, wash, and scrub for them, and not feel guilty. Which Italian women, Rose? Morgan asks, very scornful of my simplicity. 'A tiny uppercrust minority ... in the south the women live like animals.'

But Giorgio's wife is a very fine animal, a gleaming granite unchipped animal disguised as a fine woman ... and then why Patsy? No, Patsy is another story ... which other story? There isn't any other story, there's no choice about the story you find yourself in the middle of. I can only be in the middle of this one and the words have got too short to understand. No one is using words any more. Everyone is moving in shorthand, feeling in shorthand, and I never learnt it.

Then get out, Rose Williams ... get out fast while you can see. But I can't see at all well, even for getting out ... one eye is closing up and all these places are so dark.

The girl lent me the bus time-table, but I couldn't understand it. It kept missing hours or days ... sliding up and down the page in long arrows of decision which put paid to Tuesday either way. If you started from New

152

York on Wednesday you would be in Taos on Saturday. Or if from San Francisco the same, or almost. Change at Saint Louis either way. But I couldn't tell which day or which hour, whichever way I held it up. This country goes on for too many days.

I blundered back to the motel and lay down again to recover. Soon I'd have the strength to get up, to pack, to find out from someone practical about the bus.

We were digging in the sandhills; the smaller children, the cousins from Shrewsbury, had made a tunnel ... a big, big tunnel. They crawled right inside and showed me, it was a cave, a hiding-place. Aunt Wyn and Uncle Davey lay in the sun (the sun? what was the sun doing there in memory?) or out of the wind, out of sight, out of the way of the golf course.

'Rose,' Janet said, 'your legs are longer, please go in and kick it farther for us.'

So I went in ... feet first, well into the tunnel, and it came down on me up to my neck, heavy and steady, a soft prison. The cousins danced and laughed in front of me as if they had caught an elephant.

'You look so *funny!*'

'Just your face sticking out.'

I worked my shoulders free and got my hands out too.

'Don't you realize, any of *you* going in the other way with your heads down would have suffocated and died?'

'Like being bombed out?'

'Just like.'

The war was not long over.

'Come out then, Rose. Quick!'

'I can't.'

'Kick hard and come out.'

I feebly pushed my legs. The weight on them grew heavier. I began to be frightened my ribs would crack.

'You'll have to be A.R.P. people with your spades. Janet in the middle, Bill and Bobby try each side.'

Probably the first time I put on that re-assuring 'Let's all try together' teacher's voice. They rallied to it, but it took them ten minutes' silent digging. Aunt Wyn walked round the corner of the sandhill calling: 'Come and have tea, then,' just as they released me:

'Having a nice game, children? Rub the sand off your hands.'

Brisk and cheerful, quite unconscious of her children's escape from death. No one said anything about the sand trap. We sat in a furtive row avoiding each other's eyes, eating tomato sandwiches.

But I felt all the sand on me now and for ever, heavy and soft ... soft and heavy and sore in the eyes.

When I woke this second time they were both in the room. I could hear them talking above my head:

'It seems a shame to wake the poor thing,' Patsy thoughtful for my comfort.

'It should be done ... we have still some way.'

'It's a good road.'

'We should be there in light to find your house.'

'I know my own house, Giorgio.'

'I must see in light, also, the Santa Fé trail for my son.'

I stiffened, waiting for Giorgio to wake me roughly. But he did not pinch me (because Patsy was watching?), he put his hand on my hair and touched my eyelids.

'Rose, we are going now.'

'So I hear. It was good of you to wait for me.'

'How do you mean?'

Patsy was in the bathroom collecting jars of cream and her toothbrush.

'I thought you'd have gone by now.'

'Are you mad?'

'I don't know.'

'Get up and tidy your hair. It looks terrible. Why did you lie down in your dress? The linen is all creased. You should always take off your clothes to lie down.'

'Yes, Giorgio.'

'Even if I am not there.'

'I'll try to remember.'

'Now prepare yourself.'

When he had gone I bundled my things away and reached the car only a few minutes after Patsy, but it was already too late to ride next to Giorgio. I banged the door viciously, and leant half out of the window.

'I suppose somebody paid?'

'Stop that, Rose.'

'Stop what?'

'That harsh voice.'

'I won't say another word.'

'Better not.'

Better not indeed have spoken. Giorgio's irritation started him down the Santa Fé trail at a speed I dared not register ... as if we were flying from the Indians, as if an Indian crouched behind each quivering sage bush, and waited, arrows poised, on each outcrop of red rock.

'Oh, please, Giorgio!'

'What is the matter *now?*'

'Not so fast.'

'We are late. For you we became late.'

'Don't tease her,' Patsy said. 'It doesn't matter how late.'

'I wanted to see the Rio Grande,' I said. 'And the valleys of peach trees.'

'You have only to look.'

'A bit later on we run alongside the river all the way,' Patsy told me.

'If he goes this speed we'll make the river small to vanishing point.'

'But it is small here.'

'You won't know what to say to Janni, Giorgio.'

'I know how to talk to my own son.'

'I mean to tell him what you saw. You won't even have seen it.'

But as suddenly as he started he stopped, swerving the car up off the main road at Ranchos de Taos and jamming on the brakes two inches from the adobe wall round the church.

'But, Giorgio ... you said we weren't going to see any churches in America.'

'And why not?'

'But you said it yourself ... you said you saw enough churches at home.'

'You said – you said ... you are a very tiresome woman. Why do you always tie me to the past? I have forgotten what I said three weeks ago. You expect every person to react always to one pattern.'

He slammed out of the car and hurried after Patsy, already disappearing inside the church. I closed my still hurting eyes, St Francis would understand. St Francis is for the birds ... and the dogs and cats and little children. But he won't expect this tiresome insensitive woman to visit at his shrine.

'I wonder if I might look at your map?'

The other window of the car was suddenly full of face, kindly, intelligent, apologetic face. I blinked at it and the man smiled back.

'I hope you weren't really asleep?'

'Only shutting my eyes.'

I passed him the map.

'I'm not an expert tourist,' he told me. 'I like to follow my hunches, but I think there must be a better way to Santa Fé than this main highway.'

'Where are you going?'

'In the end to the Huntington Library in California. What do you think of the church?'

I looked at it ... buttresses of pinky white mud against a flawless sky.

'Very fine.'

'You're from England, aren't you?'

'More or less.'

'I was over last summer chasing George Herbert. I'm not surprised you don't find this church worth stepping out in the dust for.'

'Oh, it's not that, really. I think it's lovely.'

'I'm afraid we can't help being proud of it. We have so little seventeenth century to boast of ... but have you seen any New England churches?'

'Not yet ... perhaps when we get back over that side.'

'Some of those white wood seashore villages are quite perfect.'

'We find the West very exciting ... it's so different for us.'

He glanced at my left hand.

'That was your husband just got out of the car?'

'That's the idea.'

'I'm so glad you were both able to come to the States. I was disappointed to find in England how many people had no interest at all in anything here except the motion-picture industry.'

'I am afraid we are still very insular.'

'You know, you should take this road.'

He pointed to a wiggle on the map.

'Which road?'

'Back a little to the fork and then off into the hills through Penitentes country, and so down here to Santa Fé.'

He opened the car door and sat down beside me.

'I'm sorry I don't know how to work the air conditioning.'

I pushed a knob or two. He had on a very crisp white shirt and I was afraid it might go limp. The bow tie was a mistake and looked particularly out of place in sage brush country, but the gentle politeness came like a long cool drink. I longed to keep him talking with a flow of soft words which did not even scratch the surface.

'What will you do in California?'

'Research and more research ... but I'm on vacation now. I am ashamed to realize how little I, too, know of my own country. Would you believe it, this is my first trip West? I always took my vacations in Europe till now. Out on the eastern seaboard we feel ourselves more drawn to your side of the water than to our own deserts.'

'I love your deserts.'

What made me say that? Hating every day, every dry minute since we came down off the iris pastures of the Rockies. And I've seen nothing yet.

'Which way are you headed?'

'We are aiming to get down into Mexico.'

'Plenty more desert after Albuquerque.'

'I look forward to that … who or what are the Penitentes, anyway?'

What could they be doing together so long inside that mud edifice? Had Giorgio backed her up against the altar? Were they plotting to drop me off at the next lonely garage?

'The Penitentes? They came up into New Mexico … a Spanish sect at the end of the sixteenth century … they believe in redemption through suffering.'

That's what Giorgio is then, a Penitente.

'Whose suffering?'

Because whose redemption is Giorgio working at with his petty sadism?

'Their own, naturally; they used to flog themselves up at the top of the hills at Easter and crucify one of their number at the top.'

'How did they decide who to crucify?'

'Always plenty of volunteers…'

'Volunteers?'

'It must have been the biggest certainty of redemption of all, think of it … straight from the cross up into the flaming heavens.'

'I thought hell was the place for flames.'

'Haven't you seen a sunset yet in this part of the world? ... the lonely crosses still stand on the tops of the hills, they say.'

'But they don't use them any more?'

'Who knows? Legally, no, but people who tried to watch the Easter procession disappeared. There was a general impression they'd been shot. No one tries to watch any more.'

'Oh, we must go there.'

'You do that ... tell your husband I said so. Bob Robertson from Yale.'

'I'm Rose Williams ... from Cardiff, Wales.'

'Pleased to have met you, Rose ... why don't you and your husband have dinner with me this evening in Santa Fé?'

'I don't know exactly ... when or even whether – we shall–'

'Call me at this number.'

He scribbled on the back of a postcard and handed it to me.

'In case you get there in any shape to eat before nine o'clock.'

'Thank you ... thank you very much,' I called out after him as he got out and went over to his own Zephyr.

'Don't forget to ask them to let you see the death-cart,' he called back. 'A friend of mine saw a skeleton sitting in it.'

My mouth felt all strange from smiling. I

161

hadn't smiled for days.

He waved as he drove off, and turned right on the main road, presumably on his way up into the backwoods.

'What was that man?' asked Giorgio suspiciously.

I stayed firm in the middle and they had to get back in on each side of me.

'He only wanted to look at our map.'

'Why does he not have his own map?'

'He didn't say.'

'All Americans have their own maps.'

'How do you know? Anyway, he didn't do ours any harm, just breathing on it.'

'Why were you waving him?'

'He waved me.'

'No need to wave back.'

'Only an old-world courtesy.'

'And where was he going?'

'California.'

'This is not the way to California … what to do?'

'Oh, Giorgio, stop it, why all these questions?'

'I tell you why … because when I go in the church you are a dark sullen mess of thunder, and when I come out it is like the sun shining. You should not be so moody.'

Patsy smiled at me as if she thought I had every right to be moody if I wanted. I wondered if she expected me to hit Giorgio as we had heard her hit Ted. There was nothing handy, unless I ran round the back and got a spanner. I could take off my shoe, but we were sitting too cramped to get a good swing on it. I began to laugh.

'Why do you laugh? I am not making jokes.'

'He had such a silly idea, that man. *He's* going straight down to Santa Fé, but just because we are foreigners he thought we should go around a lot of small roads and take twice as long just to see some old crosses.'

Giorgio looked interested at once.

'What old crosses?'

'Just empty crosses, stuck on hill-tops, where they used to crucify people at Easter.'

'What people?'

'A Spanish sect ... the Penitentes.'

'Ah – I know of them.'

'I told him you weren't interested in old America–'

'Why do you tell him that?'

'That you only want to see new things.'

'You are talking nonsense ... which way is this?'

'Right here and back to the fork ... but you don't want to waste time on old suffering.'

'How do you know on what I want to waste time?'

'There's nothing there to see now,' Patsy said.

'Oh, come on, Giorgio, let's get back to

Patsy's home.'

It worked like magic, so easily I laughed again, as Giorgio, still scowling, roared the car up the side-road only about five minutes behind the Zephyr.

'Why ever did you get a convertible, Giorgio?'

'Excuse me?'

'Can't we have the roof down? You are wasting the sun.'

'No. The sun is treacherous.'

Beautiful round white close sun. Beautiful flat blue far sky and here we go back up into the hills again round and up and up and round and those deep pine woods silent with dreaming wolves.

We stopped for coffee an hour later at Penasco, a small village, everyone speaking Spanish as if we had crossed into South America.

Giorgio asked about crosses and their faces went blank ... he tried them in American, Italian and what he assured us was Spanish. They gave us directions to a church, but when we followed their road it led nowhere, only farther up into lonely black hills, the trees growing dark and close away to the sky, but the ground lit with waxy yellow flowers.

'No crosses ... he was joking ... fooling you, your man.'

'I don't think this can be the right road.'

'Gives me the shivers,' Patsy said. 'All shut

in ... I didn't know it was wild like this so close to home. Let's go back.'

She looked miserable for the first time.

Giorgio turned round and tried another road and we came to a church at Las Trampas, a sleeping empty village with only a chipmunk waiting bright-eyed on a rock.

The church was locked, we rattled the handle and peered through the enormous keyhole. A little girl came up on quiet bare feet and gave Giorgio the key without a word. She did not smile when he patted her head. She stood by the door while we went in. It looked an ordinary church ... whitewashed ... paintings round the altar, but nothing sinister.

'Ask about the death-cart, Giorgio.'

Giorgio asked the child in three languages again. She only shook her head, and held out her hand for the key. She took his fifty cents without comment and sat down on the step to spin the coin. She did not look up as we drove away.

'I thought you were supposed to be so good with children?'

'Excuse, please?'

'I thought children and dogs adored you?'

'Dogs? What dogs? I don't like dogs...'

'Will my Audrey be pleased to see me to-night!' exclaimed Patsy.

'Is your little girl not happy with her grandmother?'

'Oh, Audrey's the dog … she's an English sheepdog, that's why we named her Audrey. It's a real old English name, isn't it?'

We passed a cross at last quite close to the road, open, empty and public, listing to the left as if it had not been used for years … no withered flesh, no tattered hair sticking to it.

Giorgio was more interested when we came later on to a cowboy's grave. He stopped again, and made a small sketch of it to preserve for Janni.

'In Santa Fé I must buy him a cowboy outfit … complete with everything, the gun, the belt, the hat…'

'The horse?'

'Perhaps I get him a horse at home another time.'

'Won't he be frightened, like you?'

'He is never frightened. He has more sense.'

'We've had Suzy up on a horse already,' Patsy said. 'She thinks it's just great.'

Who did she imagine this Janni we talked about was, anyway? Some nephew? She did not ask, with tact or without interest. She began to talk about Suzy, as if coming into the child's wavelength made her more real. How she didn't sleep well at night, cried always two or three times, drove Ted crazy in hot weather, woke in the dawn and sang, like an out-of-tune bird. Ted once put a sack over her head in a rage as if she were a canary, but that only made her worse, she screamed then as well, high and long.

Evening

Santa Fé arrived out of hot pink towering rocks and the endless measly spotted bushes of the plain. Patsy glowed with joy at her return. I tried to see it with her eyes as 'home', but to me it was just a large commercial town, all competing gas stations, row upon row of motels, whimsy false adobe walls, bleak, tawdry – and dry.

'Could we stop near the centre, please?' Patsy asked. 'I'll call Ted's mother and have her bring Suzy over, and I've some things to get. Will you two kind people have supper with us tonight?'

'I don't think...' I began doubtfully, but to my surprise Giorgio was much more definite.

'No, thank you ... not tonight ... some other time when we return.'

Perhaps he reckoned Ted would have calmed down by then.

He drew up near the post office.

'We wait here for you,' he told Patsy.

'I'll be right with you.' She jumped out.

'Rose – make the parking meter to work,' Giorgio ordered. 'I do not understand it.'

When I had set the meter I got back in and

we were alone for the first time that day. His head fell back against the seat.

'I have a 'orrible headache.'

'Horrible ... with an H.'

'I am speaking French. What is the matter with you, always correcting me? You should enjoy me how I am.'

'I am my own worst enemy.'

'It is true. Why are you treating me so badly?'

'I like *that* ... *I* treat you badly? What about...?'

'Why don't you stroke the back of my neck? I like *that.*'

His hair grew very thick low down on his head.

'Where is your neck, anyway?'

He guided my fingers to the top of his spine.

'Now, very gently ... you have soft fingers for so hard a woman.'

'But I thought you said my hands were like sandpaper?'

'Why do you always listen to what I say? And remember it also?'

'How else can I find out what you think?'

'But I never say what I think ... you must approach people round corners ... obliquely ... never straightforward. You walk straight forward, and you crush all the little flowers underfoot.'

'But I particularly didn't ... when we...'

'You make me very tired,' he sighed.

'*I* make you tired.' I stopped stroking his neck. '*I* do ... when you were out dancing for hours with Patsy ... how can you say that to me? No wonder you are tired ... a stout, middle-aged man trying to jive and keep up with a girl of twenty.'

'At least she is a mother ... not an old schoolgirl like you.'

He got out of the car in a sudden rush.

'Giorgio ... where are you going? Giorgio!'

'It is the post office,' he called. 'Perhaps I will have a letter.'

He started across the road, head down, following his big nose, not looking right or left while the cars braked noisily for him. I ran after him more slowly, waiting for the Fords to pass, not wanting to lose my legs and have to go to Aldermaston in a wheelchair.

'There is no need to kill yourself for a letter.'

'But I must know if she is all right now.'

At Taos Giorgio's wife had been lying down a good deal with a slight touch of the gripe. There had been no one to look after her in her distress except her mother, her aunt, Giorgio's sister, Giorgio's aunt, and three or four domestics all rendered incompetent by unhappy personal problems.

This time Giorgio had two letters and I, at last, one. I held it in my hand hard and heavy without opening it and watched the open country of Giorgio's changing face.

'Ah ... thank God, she is better ... but now it is the children! What a terrible summer for her! I should never have gone away. The sun is not even shining and the sea is strangely rough. The fishermen are all bewildered. It is the fault of de Gaulle and his bomb of *Gloire*. He has ruined the Mediterranean. Now perhaps we shall also have another earthquake.'

He looked at me, his eyes suddenly big and dark with catastrophe.

'Nonsense, Giorgio! They don't have earthquakes in Italy.'

'Yes, they did before ... tidal waves also.'

'You are thinking of Greece.'

'You should see Pompeii and the twisted fossil of the old men who could not get away from the rushing sea of hot lava.'

'But in any case she is not near Naples.'

'It could be dangerous ... and there are riots now in Genova. That is quite near. Perhaps the fascists come back to power and I am again all the time in jail. With my poor health that would not be good. When I think of prison I am no longer a young man.'

He drooped against the counter.

I opened Morgan's letter. He too was thinking about going to jail. A split and quarrelling Labour Party was paralysed. He had reluctantly decided that he would now have to join the Direct Action branch of the Nuclear Disarmers. Kruschev would not wait five years for the Labour Party to have another, even slighter, chance of coming to power. Even the Chinese were not rooting for the British Labour Party. So he was off to roll in the mud at the next rocket-site demonstration, and might well be serving his first six months by the time I got home. Meanwhile, the woman in the flat below was giving him supper all right, but it was a useful preparation for prison fare and the sooner I came back to give him a good send-off the better. He was sorry he would probably lose his job over it, but he counted on me to keep earning for the time being, and bring him home-baked cakes to pass through the bars. He preferred chocolate with an occasional fruit-cake. He was as usual very busy, but he missed me ... particularly at meal times, and loved me, and must now get back to the pile of exam papers on his table.

Giorgio had been watching my face.

'Why are you smiling now?' he asked.

'Morgan is going to prison also.'

'In England? Not possible ... so free a country for politics and so quiet. No one cares there in any case. What are these?'

He pulled out of my hand the photographs Morgan had sent, taken at Morgan's sister's house in Barry when their baby was christened. There was one of Morgan under an

171

apple tree waving his arms and yelling at his poor Christian Tory brother-in-law who will never be a capitalist as long as he lives, and only wants to live quietly, going in to work in the bank every morning, and mowing his tiny mortgaged lawn of a Saturday. The sort of man very liable to be shot in a bank robbery protesting that he never did believe in violence. Morgan bullies him and I've seen Tom's hand shake on the teapot when Morgan raises his voice too far. There was another photograph of me leaning over the cradle. I didn't like the look on my face. It wasn't sentimental, more sly and greedy. It's an ugly baby, quite bald with a squint, and in my conscious moments I don't want it a bit. Luckily Morgan's sister doesn't seem to notice its looks.

'I don't like it.'

Giorgio glared at the photographs.

'Don't like what?'

'He looks big and strong, but he takes no notice of you. It is not right. You should leave him.'

'He often does notice me. He just happened to be arguing with Tom. It was so typical of them both I took it when they weren't looking.'

'I take care of my wife all the time. Every minute of the day. She is very patient with me.'

'So you said…'

Over Giorgio's shoulder I saw the Yale man go up to the counter and ask for mail. I tried to crouch down, to put Giorgio's back between him and me.

Giorgio put his hand out to me.

'What is the matter? You have pain in the stomach?'

By now I was almost on the floor, scratching a mosquito bite on my ankle, but it was no good.

'Why, hullo there!... If it isn't Mr and Mrs Williams. So you made it, then?'

Bob Robertson's big kind face smiled all over. Giorgio did not smile back.

'Yes, thank you ... Bob ... Giorgio.'

'Giorgio? That certainly sounds a fine old Tudor name... Did your family go over to mine coal?'

'Excuse me?'

He shook Giorgio's unoffered hand heartily.

'We followed your inland route,' I broke in quickly.

'Good ... good ... you found the way, then?'

'We found it all right, but the death-cart had disappeared.'

'Oh dear. I regret if I raised your hopes too much.'

'Oh, it didn't matter ... it didn't matter at all. We had a very nice ride. Didn't we, Giorgio?'

'Excuse, please?'

'Shall I have the pleasure of seeing you later?'

Bob asked me, giving up the attempt to get through to Giorgio.

'I'm afraid I don't know yet ... we haven't even checked in.'

I looked at Giorgio for support, but his eyes clouded with blankness. Any minute he would begin humming *Traviata*.

'Give me a call when you are ready, then,' Bob said. 'I'd be glad to show you the town. The English were very good to me last year.'

'Thank you ... that's very kind.'

He shook my hand equally heartily, and strode out of the post office, in a glow of baffled good will.

'He is paying court to you,' Giorgio growled.

'Don't be ridiculous. He only just met me.'

'It is enough.'

'He's only being kind. To both of us. Americans are very kind.'

'He is not kind to me. He has nearly broken my wrist.'

'You should not have resisted his handshake.'

'He exaggerates.'

We were both standing with one arm on the counter, and a fat man coming up to buy some stamps brushed me against Giorgio.

For a moment we were together. Giorgio was shivering. He put his arm out to steady me and dug his nails into my shoulder.

'You see?'

I could only see his fierce, close face.

'Oh, Rose, try to understand.'

But I do try all the time, I try too hard. I can't stop thinking. I can't stop worrying. I can't let things slip slide take their frantic course. I just don't know what you are talking about ... I don't think it's the English, American, French, Italian lack of communication. It seems that this old schoolgirl is a severe case of frozen adolescence. With my idiotic good nature I never learnt this complicated other language of love. I'm getting out of this love country where the inhabitants speak gibberish and move in arabesques.

'Giorgio ... I think I'll go back from here. I'll take the bus or maybe even the train.'

'No ... no, not possible.' He gripped my wrist.

'If Morgan's going to prison he needs me.'

'I need you more.'

'Patsy can read the map for you.'

'Patsy – Patsy ... what is Patsy?'

'Well – you tell me ... what is Patsy?'

'A silly little girl ... one of my not-to-be-touched students.'

'But very pretty...'

'Of course she is very pretty. The world is full of very pretty girls. It is a happy circumstance ... not only in Italy, but whenever I travel I find this to be true. You should be pleased.'

'Oh, please let me go.'

'No. I love you.'

'It's a foreign language ... you don't know what you are saying. It doesn't mean anything to you in English...'

I pulled my hand away and flung myself at the door. My heel caught and I arrived in the hot street on my face. I sat on the sidewalk rocking my empty heart, and moaning: 'Oh, no ... no ... no...' meaning no help in the blue sky, betrayed by shoe manufacturers and post offices, unable to make even a dignified departure from agony.

'What are you doing?' Giorgio asked with interest, crouching down beside me.

'Resting ... taking the weight off my feet.'

'You should not sit in the street.'

'You sit down, too. Keep me in countenance. The pavement is warm.'

He held out my shoe. I looked at it sadly, now without a heel and two inches shorter than the other. I took off the first and handed it to him. The people of Santa Fé walked busily past us to and fro and fro and to.

'You see, it doesn't matter sitting here. No one is calling a cop. Why don't you get me a little go-cart, Giorgio, and I could shuffle along like Porgy and make some money singing "Summertime"?'

'The sun has got inside your head.'

'Lovely golden brains ... do you remember being happy?'

'What are you talking now about? Get up...'

'Can't.'

He dragged me to my feet. To my foot. The other one was made of electrified iron filings. I felt sick with pain.

'I am loving you all the time, Rose.'

'There's nice.'

'You should feel this ... words are not necessary.'

'Or deeds either?'

He was half-carrying me again.

'Why do you have such weak feet? British women are supposed to be very strong in the foot ... frigid but footstrong. We export to Britain many great big shoes.'

'I don't normally have weak feet. When we are on holiday Morgan and I go for long walks ... all over the place.'

'You should not. It makes you thick ankles.'

'But you liked my ankles before.'

'They are all right to look at, but why is that every time I speak sweetly to you you fall down?'

'It's the shock.'

'It is very inconvenient. I shall not pay you any more compliments.'

I rubbed my face against his silk shirt as he

dumped me back in the car. He was panting badly.

'It is not good for me to lift you. You should consider my health.'

'Why?'

'Because I want you.'

'You do? What a delicious surprise.'

I moved my mouth away from his.

'Do not be coquette with me.'

'Isn't that what Italian women do?'

He pulled me back against him by the hair. American cars are well arranged with no brake or gear levers to get in the way. I breathed cool silk with his body hard against my thigh.

'Oh, Rose, touch me.'

'Not now, Giorgio … you're mad.'

'Just a little … just gently.'

'It'll be worse … darling, don't. We'll be arrested or something.'

'America is not Italy. It is the land of Henry Miller. Love me!'

I twisted my head to see Patsy, her arms full of two enormous grocery bags, opening the car door.

'Hi, love birds!' she trilled. 'I certainly hope Ted's that pleased to see *me*.'

Giorgio shook himself like a dog coming to shore.

'Impossible to drive at this moment,' he muttered in French. 'Why do you do this to me?'

He put his head down on the steering-wheel. I tried to distract Patsy with house-wifely chat about frozen goods as she climbed into the back to keep her parcels steady. I found I was shaking myself, so I kept my hands low, out of sight.

'Don't touch me!' Giorgio hissed.

'Wouldn't dream of it.'

'*Allons-y!*' Patsy cried, leaning forward and patting Giorgio's shoulder. 'The ice-cream's melting, and I want you to see my place before the sun goes down.'

Giorgio started the car with vicious jumps, swearing in what I recognized by now as Roman dialect.

'What's he saying?' Patsy asked me.

'I don't know.'

'Does he know any Moulin Rouge love songs?'

'Do you know any Moulin Rouge love songs, Giorgio?'

'I cannot sing at all.'

'He cannot sing at all, I'm afraid, Patsy.'

'Ted sings, with his guitar. Old choirboy and chain gang songs, makes me sad. Will you stay just a little while, you two? He won't go off the deep end with you there. His mother's coming with Suzy, too. It'll be quite a party.'

Patsy's blue eyes were sharper, with fear or anticipation, than I'd seen them so far.

I looked at Giorgio humming *Traviata*

again to the mud-walled suburbs. He gave no sign he'd heard her.

'I expect so,' I told her soothingly. 'We're in no hurry.'

She had directed Giorgio off the main high road and we were now turning right and left in a maze of secret houses. They were all pinky-brown, all low, all protected by walls nearly as high as themselves. Bursts of purple Bougainvillaea over the smooth mud-plastered walls betrayed the gardens inside.

Patsy told him to stop the car by a wrought-iron gate. I wondered for a moment if Giorgio would get out at all, he was giving a good imitation of a spent oarsman at the end of a hard race, but Patsy had noticed nothing, she was tripping up her front path, behind her groceries, calling her child.

I risked touching Giorgio's cheek as it rested on the wheel.

'Don't you feel well?'

'How can you ask that? You know how I feel.'

'It is only for a little while. Just come in for a minute.'

'You go ... I wait here.'

'But there's her luggage.'

He pulled himself out of the car ... snatched her case from the back, and followed me up the path groaning in Roman numerals.

'Giorgio, don't ... what will she think?'

'Why do I care what she thinks?'

'There's her mother, too, and Ted.'

'That Ted will kill me. One blow in my liver and I am totally dead.'

'Not in front of his mother.'

'More so because of his mother – to prove he is strong.'

'Well, perhaps he won't guess *where* to hit you.'

'What does it matter where he hits me?'

'I thought it was only your liver that was vulnerable.'

'*Un coup* or *quatre cents coups* are all the same to an Italian. We are too civilized for violence.'

'Probably Ted is civilized, too.'

'He did not sound civilized at that motel. Anyway, he is an American.'

The front door was wide open. We tracked down Patsy's happy laughter in a dream kitchen. She had the baby sitting on the table and was hugging it and talking to Ted's trim, tidy, collected, not-much-more-than-forty mother. No sign of Ted.

Patsy swung the baby round on to her knee and sat on the table herself, while she introduced us and explained how good we had been to her.

'That *boy!*' said Ted's mother with proud disapproval. 'Wait till I tell him.'

'I made sure he'd be back.' But Patsy did

not look disturbed.

'Not a *word*,' said his mother gaily, delighted by her son's fine independence.

'I'll miss the station wagon, though,' Patsy remarked.

'I'll call every morning,' Mrs Ted promised, drawing on her neat, white gloves.

Giorgio had straightened up at the good news of Ted's absence, and began to wander round the kitchen stroking the gadgets.

'This would be good for my wife.'

He sprang back nervously as he set off a turning electric spit with a soft whirr.

'But you say she is never in the kitchen, Giorgio?'

'If she had all this ... she would go there. It is not nice there now, so she stays away.'

'But then you would put the domestics out of work.'

'No, no, they could do other things. There is always much, with three children.'

'Come and see our pool.'

Patsy put her arm through his, and guided him out of the kitchen door into the garden. Ted's mother followed, yelling news of Suzy's latest sleeping habits.

Suddenly the baby and I were alone in the Ideal Home. It did not cry for its mother or its grandmother, though it wriggled round on the table and put out one fat arm hopefully towards them. Its eyes were as blue as Patsy's in a face even rounder than hers.

182

'Hi, there!' I tried handing it a finger.

To my surprise it took hold and bit tentatively.

'You're a monkey ... just a monkey.'

It giggled and chewed my thumb as well.

'Well, what's the difference? Sorry, I didn't bring any nuts.'

I crouched down and put my hands right round it. It was as stout and pink as a sucking-pig in its frilly gingham sun-suit, so much poundage of delicious flesh. It leant forward staring solemnly at me until its nose hit mine, then it giggled again and hurled itself off the table into my arms. I overbalanced and sat back hard on the floor with my lap full of baby. I was wrong about the flesh. She was a person after all, screaming with laughter at her own small cruel joke.

'Monster ... monkey monster!' I told her.

She put her hands over her eyes and laughed through her fingers.

I dragged myself up by the dish-washer, steadying her on one hip.

'Out!' she shrieked like an angry parrot, kicking her plump heels into my thigh.

'You bet we're going out ... I don't trust you.'

We appeared in the doorway, framed in oleander, as Giorgio and Patsy turned to come back up the garden. For a second his face softened into the same tenderness he usually kept for letter-reading in the post office. I had a wild idea he might rush forward and make some irrevocable demonstration of love even in front of witness Patsy. I stayed there waiting hopefully feeling like the Spartan boy, because although to Giorgio the light curled back of Suzy's head lay gently on my breast, she was all the time snitching the soft inside part of my arm with her clever new teeth. But nothing happened. Giorgio took a step towards me, said, 'Rose,' in a doubtful voice, as if not sure it was me at all, and then turned back politely to Patsy. Suzy squirmed fiercely in my arms, squeaking, 'Down … down … down,' and when I let her go tottered along the path to her mother's legs.

Patsy swung her up, and the pretty picture, Giorgio's Complete Woman, woman with child, was repeated nearer to him with a background of falsely blue pool water.

I was left rubbing the red tooth-marks on my arm and making polite remarks to Ted's mother who was telling me how Ted and Patsy had been childhood sweethearts, and walking out together since they were six and eight years old, and how they were still only a couple of kids and quarrelled like kids, and what a wonderful time their own kids would have growing up with them, all kids together. I sat down on the step – my ankle hurt badly now – and leant back against Patsy's mud house, it felt oddly cool … it was cool inside, too, come to think of it, or was that air-conditioning? Mrs Ted seemed to be going, she guessed Ted would be back any time, thought they'd both like to be together for the big reunion.

'It always ends up the same way, and it can't be too soon for Ted,' she told me with what, on any less good and clean-cut face, would have seemed a leer. Mrs Ted's efficient kindness filtered it through as an amiable hint.

'Giorgio,' I called, 'we should be going.'

Giorgio ruffled the baby's silky hair ... it was clear he would have liked to do the same for Patsy.

She saw us all off at the gate, melting into the distance with the baby still in her arms, a symphony of golden pink gingham and flesh and mud in a wide pinky gold Santa Fé sunset.

'Well done, St Christopher!'

I rubbed my head against his shoulder, relaxing for the first time since that Eagle Nest.

'Don't touch me.' He edged away.

'*Now* what have I done?'

'First we must find somewhere to go.'

'And then?'

'Then I love you very much ... till you are not breathing ... then we go out and eat a very big dinner.'

'That'll be hard work if I'm not breathing.'

'I will eat for you … and drink, too.'

'And then?'

'Guess.'

'Lovely Indian bird dances?'

'No…'

'Tour of Santa Fé night spots? Gambling?'

'No … try again.'

'I give up … it's too difficult.'

'Then we go back to bed, of course, and I love you again until at last we go to sleep. And tonight we shall sleep very well.'

He began to sing like Papageno, a jerky bird-song … love in Italian makes the world go round. No wonder the world's in such a shaky state, and going squarer every day. I hummed with him, not knowing the words. We came out in the short dusk on the main highway with hundreds of motels flashing their neon signs on each side of the road.

'How shall we choose?' he asked.

'The first with palm trees.'

'I don't like palm trees. They remind me of the campaign in Africa.'

'I thought you never fought?'

'Later … it became necessary. I had my mother to think of.'

'But you were in prison.'

'That was before. You should listen to what I say.'

'Then the first with a swimming pool … we can swim in the dark.'

'That would not be good for my health.'

'In the morning, then.'

'Perhaps ... I think I take the seventh on the left – the side of the heart.'

'Not *that* side...'

'*Uno, due, trios, quatre,* five, six, *now...*'

'Oh, *no,* Giorgio ... don't ... don't ... you'll never get over that side of the road.'

I shut my eyes as he swung across the lights of the vast automobile batting down to Albuquerque, and opened them again as we screeched, still alive and laughing, into a courtyard of adobe Swiss chalets.

'Oh, Giorgio ... you'll be the death of me ... what about *my* health ... *my* heart?'

'*You?* You are strong for anything.'

Tonight his American was fluent and sufficient. He paid his eight dollars for a chalet, parked the car at our new front door, pushed me over the threshold, and began to kiss me leaning against the end of the one big bed.

'The door, darling ... it's wide open ... the light ... the car lights – the luggage.'

'Do not be so practical.'

But he let me go suddenly and I toppled backwards on to the bed.

He had already gone out and was slamming the car doors. I propped myself up on the pillow and watched him bring in his own case.

'Get undressed,' he told me. 'Do not lie about like that. I have told you before. You spoil your dress.'

He came back again with my case and a small basket. He held this up for me to see.

'Is this yours?'

'No ... what a bore ... it's Patsy's.'

'I take it back then.' He pulled on his jacket.

'What, *now?*'

I sat up bereft and indignant, and altogether disbelieving.

'I am only gone ten minutes... Time for you to undress. Better now than in the morning when that Ted is there to kill me.'

'Oh, Giorgio ... I can't bear it.'

'What is the matter? You make your eyes so big.'

'Kiss me first.'

'It is only ten minutes.'

'Please ... just once before you go.'

'No ... not at all.' He backed away to the door. 'Otherwise I cannot manage to drive at all, as you well know.'

'Let's send it to her,' I called. 'We're always in a post office.'

But he had already started the engine.

I got up and drew the curtains across. It took one minute, not ten, to remove my clothes. I wandered naked round the chalet, hanging up my dress, washing out my pants and bra. I looked at the empty bed, but it seemed foolish to get into it alone so early in the evening. I turned off the air-conditioning which was making me shiver and decided to have a bath. I left the front door on the latch so that Giorgio could get in without me, the key still lay on the table beside the ever-present Bible. The American Bible Society must be the busiest in the world.

I lay in the bath a long time, putting my sore ankle up on the edge to take the pressure off it. It was swelling up nicely, by morning it would be useless. I wondered if poor Morgan were in prison yet, I guessed he would wait till the end of the school term. He is such a responsible man that even if he planned martyrdom he would give his headmaster time to find a replacement first. I would not get another letter till we reached Mexico City. The woman downstairs never was much of a cook, she probably bought fish and chips on the corner four days out of seven. She was busy giving Morgan an ulcer. Why doesn't he worry about me? Couldn't he get an ulcer that way, worrying what I'm at? Why does he trust me to the ends of the earth? Does he think no one else will ever look at me anyway?

When the bath feels too chilly I get out and rub myself with a silly small towel and put on Giorgio's red silk robe for comfort. He must feel like a king inside here. And the time? How is the time getting along on its own? How big is that ten minutes now? Maybe my watch stopped. Except that it stopped an hour ahead, not an hour behind, and it's ticking hard. Well, an hour's not much, allowing for a quick drink for old times' sake. But what's he doing having a quick drink with Patsy instead of me? Bathing the baby? Roasting a chicken? A quick dip in the new pool? Come out and smell the moonlit oleanders? *Do* they smell?

I got into bed with the Bible. It was company and there's no doubt it's a good book … not *the* Good Book but *a* good book, full of rattling good yarns like Potiphar's wife and Benjamin and poor old Ruth. I wish I were a Jew holding together across their deserts so long and for sure, making home in their heads all those centuries. Or an American able to accept and adapt and turn an Italian into a good Bostonian. Anyone but me failing on all counts, nationally and naturally, sitting here alone in red silk reading St Paul's Epistle to the Romans. No clue to my Roman here:

'I beseech you, brethren, by the mercies of God that ye present your bodies a living sacrifice, holy, acceptable unto God which is your reasonable service.'

Where's the reason in all this with two hours gone and half Revelation and no sweetness in the Song of Songs?

Night

At ten o'clock I rang Bob Robertson. He sounded politely surprised. He had written off the Williamses and eaten supper an hour ago. Did we still want to see the town? I wanted to see people, human beings, Americans ... but I told him I was hungry and my husband had broken down, out of town, and suggested I didn't wait for him.

Maybe he *has* broken down, cars are always doing that. Particularly cars that are visiting young deserted wives.

Bob sounded even more surprised, but he'd be glad to pick me up if I'd care to tell him where I was. I trailed the telephone across to the window and looked out at the neon sign. I seemed to be at the 'essuis al' motel. I told him this.

'El Assoose surely?' Bob suggested. 'Sounds more Mexican.'

'It doesn't *look* very Mexican. They are all shaped like chalets with sloping roofs.'

'Then you are reading it backwards.'

I put my head on one side and tried again. 'You're right.'

'I'll find it. Shouldn't be too many Swiss motels on that road.'

He hung up.

I dressed with great precision. The sweat dripped off me again but I was still shivering, my hands didn't seem to belong to the rest of the outfit, they stuck to the silk as I tried to bundle it back with Giorgio's things, and stuck to my hair going up into a Japanese knot. I had to stand on one leg all the time.

'It hurts,' I told the God of Aliens out loud, meaning my foot, meaning the emptiness, meaning everything. I watched my face crumple up for crying and the tears begin to run into the sweat. I felt sorry for my poor face, my poor foot. I even jabbed my poor head with hairpins. I must not start crying because there will be no reasonable service for stopping. Everything that is done to you ... you do. No one is against you but yourself. Loving is not enough, nobody wants love without intelligence, without cunning, without guile and creation. If Morgan is bored with you it is your fault ... you-red-ugly-sodden, hitting your head against the glass there.

I was making so much noise howling and banging about and hopping in and out with my wet underclothes to pack on top, I didn't hear the extra car drive in until Bob started shouting: 'Rose ... Rose Williams!' up and down the courtyard, and I realised I'd forgotten to say where or what name.

I opened the door and yelled, 'Here!' and hopped back and held my head under the cold shower and the sudden shock stopped the awful noise coming out of me anyway.

And I called to him in the room almost sounding like an ordinary human being, with just a heavy cold in the head:

'I won't be a moment ... just one or two last things ... hope you didn't take long to find me. *Such* a pity about my poor husband. He'll be so hungry. As a matter of fact, I'm leaving him. I hope you don't mind?'

I appeared in the bathroom doorway with my eyes bulging and my head all wrapped up in a white towel like an apoplectic Arab. I could see the poor man bewildered ... wondering which of us was dotty, or if he'd ever seen me before. He measured the distance for escape and hung on to a chair.

'Come now, Rose Williams, let me get this straight.'

'It's rather hard to get straight. It's just a sudden decision. It's been coming on for a long time.'

'You don't look too good ... maybe you should see a doctor?'

'I feel fine ... perfectly fine ... I haven't been drinking, either ... I've just been sorrowing. Sorrow takes it out of you, you know. It's not at all good for the health. Mixes up the glands in some way ... so I thought I'd give it up. Let's just be happy ... night and day all the time ... happy, like on an ocean voyage.'

He looked really scared. His bow tie was slipping.

'I think perhaps I'll come back later when you are more relaxed.'

'Oh, I'm relaxed ... hey-ho, practically on my knees ... I didn't mean you and me for the ocean voyage. Nothing personal about happiness. Just all the world ought to be. Or all the world that isn't hungry. That must be at least half the world by now. Don't you think what with U.N.O. and U.N.N.R.A. and W.F.O. and all that lot working away, don't you think they must have got about half-way for hunger. Wouldn't you say?'

The water had stopped dripping down my neck. I dabbed it off my face, too, and powdered the now enormous area of my nose.

'It's very sad,' I mourned for me. 'What sorrow has done for my nose! Look – only this morning it was at least an inch smaller. You'd hardly know it now, would you? I mean, I hardly know it myself, so I'm not surprised it looked unfamiliar to you.'

'If you haven't been drinking what you need is a drink.'

'You are extremely right, Bob Robertson. I knew I could trust you to arrange everything – but everything.'

'But my dear girl,' he blenched, if that's a mixture of paling and shrinking both at once, 'I hardly know you.'

'All the better,' try teacher's voice for size, 'for taking an impersonal view. You can't leave me here alone when the brute has driven off and left me?'

'But I thought you said *you* were going to leave *him*?'

'I see now I was wrong to tell him he was getting fat and old. He was much ruder to me ... really, you wouldn't believe some of the things he said to me, but I didn't understand the rules.'

'What rules?'

'That's the trouble. I still don't know. He never told me, but it's no doubt there were rules ... lots of rules.'

I snapped my case shut and handed it to Bob. He took it reluctantly and balanced it on the arm of the chair.

'You'll regret this ... in the morning you'll feel calmer.'

'In the morning I shall be headed back to New York.'

His face cleared. If I was so soon travelling in the opposite direction and had no wish to see California he was safe. Must be. He led the way out to his car, but started a lecture on the patience necessary to a good marriage relationship.

'And what's more, you should leave him a note, Rose.'

'Why?'

'He'll be back looking for you to say sorry and make up.'

'And when do you think that will be?'

'In the morning anyway. Then he will be desperate to know where you've gone.'

I borrowed a pen from him and left a note. On the table. Just a simple tasteful epitaph:

'Gone Home – Rose,' I wrote, and left the key for him at the motel office.

As we drove along Bob continued his lecture on Matrimony. He had never tried it himself but he had now been three years under analysis and was beginning to think in terms of a positive lasting relationship with the other sex. I took another look at him through my aching eyes ... but his gentle dead friendliness was just what I liked tonight. I had no energy left to consider his problems, let alone become involved in them. We were very well matched for the time of day.

'Where are we going?' I asked. Not caring, but to keep him talking.

'Back to my grandma's place.'

I closed my eyes and watched Giorgio against the red lids chasing Patsy in and out the gadgets in that splendid kitchen. There must be other rooms but I had not seen them. I could only imagine him catching her giggling against the ice box, the vast ice box, kiss her stretched across the white Formica table. I do not know what Giorgio looks like sitting down socially in a chair. I sat with him in drug stores and cars and lecture rooms and stood on sidewalks and in post offices. There were always only beds to sit on and then so much easier to lie. Maybe it would not have turned out like this if we could have been comfortable anywhere except in bed. A couple of folding canvas chairs on the plains of Kansas. Two hammocks in the pine trees of the Rockies. Two rockers among the desert tumbling weeds. Talking of this and that:

The lonely position of the Italian intellectual.

The superiority of Welsh mutton over veal.

The lack of communist funds to mend the town sewer.

How to get twenty children to listen in a class of forty.

The church money roaring away in fireworks.

And I don't even know the name of Giorgio's wife. Every day I could have asked him, but she was there so strong without one. No name and no face but always more alive than I was. He punished me for her and now he's punishing Patsy for me. All right, Giorgio, you needn't go on… Leave Patsy at least out of it, you felt guilty enough without adding her. Be reasonable, be quiet and Oh, be HERE.

'It was her bronchitis,' Bob was saying. 'They thought a desert winter might help with her breathing, and then she stayed on.'

But if there's Patsy too, that makes *me* less, doesn't it? Oh, Giorgio, don't take away from me ... don't minimise me out of existence. It hurts ... hurts ... I can feel the goodness seeping out of the soles of my feet.

'She made friends down here, quite settled in but my mother wanted me to be sure and look her up. Otherwise I'd have gone round by Wyoming.'

'She must have been very glad to see you.'

'Well, of course, I am her only grandchild. But she writes she's quite at home here now. We'll have a job to get her back East.'

I settled into Giorgio, nested, breathed better, treated him like a holiday camp, tried to make friends with him ... *friends,* imagine, out of my mind ... fatal. Who ever heard of such a thing? We arrived at another long low creamy-in-the-moonlight house. No lights in any windows.

'Where's Grandma?' I asked the wolf as he poured me a strong scotch.

'Watching TV in bed. I tucked her up before I went out. I'll find you something to eat in a minute. Drink up, do you good.'

I sank down on a very low divan strewn with Navaho Indian rugs. It seemed easier to take my feet off the floor and tuck them under me. When Bob went out to the kitchen I lay back in a heavy scent of what might be frangipani from the dark garden.

By now Giorgio and Patsy are swimming naked in the soft pool, then she is twining him tiny garlands of frangipani. The night air is not good for his liver and if he keeps on protectively his pants and vest, that tiny garland is going to look out of place. Of course, Lady C. stopped to slip on her rubber-soled shoes before running out in the rain, so a sufficiently high purpose or high density of passion will ward off the ridicule and the night dew. And I'm not there to spoil everything laughing. I'd laugh my head off if I *was* there. But I'm not there. Nobody asked me to the party. Anyway, he wouldn't want Patsy to see his moon-illuminated stomach at all, would he? so think the scene all over again, but indoors. Has he discreetly spread the paunch over a desert dog rug? What about that busy baby? Is she howling to the moon yet, or bringing them goblets of asses' milk?

Back in my own love-scene soft music began to waft into the room through the ceiling as Bob brought me a shrimp omelette and salad. He sat down beside me on the divan and encouraged me to eat. He need not have bothered with the encouragement as by now I felt faint with hunger, as if Giorgio had been not a holiday camp but a sanatorium from which I had recently escaped.

I shall live after all, I shall get better and

mend. There are colours and sounds and strange smells in the world, just like they say. America is a continent, not just a back-cloth for Giorgio. Tomorrow I will open my eyes and take a good look at it, so that I can tell Morgan what I saw. *Bonjour,* America, how ever did I come to take things so seriously? dignify adultery with *tristesse* and miss every mountain range and twisting river in futile explorations of one human heart, and that heart not even in very good condition.

'You know, you should go back,' Bob advised me.

'Oh, I know. Of that I am now fully aware. I'll start very first thing tomorrow.'

'No ... tonight. He'll be waiting there, for sure.'

'There's nothing for sure about Giorgio.'

'The usual behaviour pattern suggests a quick return.'

'But whose usual behaviour pattern? He doesn't have the same patterns as anyone I know.'

'I don't expect he deviates far. You are just not familiar with the range of possibilities.'

'You try and get familiar with Giorgio ... you just try, that's all.'

I chased the last shrimp with a bit of bread, American bread is so soft the crusts don't have any pushing power, and handed him the tray.

'Very good. Did you really cook it yourself?'

'I do all my own cooking ... except when I'm staying with my mother. I don't live with her any more now.'

He put the tray on the floor and leaned closer.

'How clever of you ... to cook so well,' I said.

'I've been alone a long time, Rose. I know what I'm talking about, you don't. How long have you been married, did you say?'

'I didn't... Ten years.'

'Ten? It's not possible.'

'True, though.'

'Then it's quite out of the question you leave him now in the middle of a big transcontinental trip. Why, you must have saved years for this experience.'

Was this what I was saving for all those years with Morgan? Not spending myself lavishly, economising the expense of spirit to Morgan's cost.

'We are both here on scholarship grants for post-graduates.'

This shocked him more than ever, this waste of public grant opportunity.

'I think I'll drive you back this very minute.'

But I put my hand on his shirt sleeve...

'Please, Bob ... no ... I need a breathing space. A few hours, anyway.'

He took off his glasses casually and polished them with a piece of Kleenex. He kept them in his hand after that and edged up a bit on me. I waited to feel something from the touch of his arm on my ankle. If my feet have been trained to exist on their own this is a test. I am taking my feet away to Wales, they don't belong to Giorgio. Nothing happened, not even a tingle of anticipation.

'You see, my dear,' Bob was droning on. 'It is perfectly natural that you should have these impulses to re-discovery. Extra tensions inevitably build up on a trip. You don't have the normal outlets. Now, if you were in your own house you could rage out to the kitchen and bake an angel cake or thump it off on a whole load of ironing. No children, you say? That's serious ... you need help there. Have you tried straightforward medical help? Often, if your husband is not impotent...'

'Oh, no, *that's* not the trouble at all.'

'I must admit he didn't look impotent. One can usually tell, you know.'

'Can you? How extraordinary.'

'Of course, I only saw him briefly but he struck me as a man with, to say the least, very vigorous sexual confidence. Anyway, as I was saying, *provided* he is not impotent, often the very slightest changes in the fertility rating alters the whole picture. When you get home you must undoubtedly set to work to reorganize your marriage relationship. In the very last resort adoption is often an excellent outlet for frustration.

He put his arm right round me in a protective way. I leant back against the arm … perhaps it would turn into a flying saucer to carry me over the hot sands and the cold Atlantic to my own green rain. Perhaps they're off the dog rug by now and Giorgio is carrying her into the pale pink bedroom. I'm sure it's pale pink with delicious sprigged nylon curtains. Carrying heavy weights makes him breathe hard and fast, but he can pass that off as passion.

There was some heavy breathing going on by my own left ear. I kept my eyes closed and pretended not to notice. If I am feeble enough somebody else will arrange everything, send me home in an ambulance, or even a coffin. Unfortunately, just as Bob's lips made a tentative nibble at my cheek there was an outburst of gunfire from upstairs. Evidently Grandma had changed over to a late-night Western.

'I *told* her to keep to the serenade,' Bob sounded very irritated.

He pulled his arm away and left me to slump back on the cushions. I could hear him calling to her as he ran upstairs.

I didn't wait for the argument. The whisky and the shrimps had given me strength. I picked up my case from the hall and walked out into the darkness which now seemed to smell of old sheep rather than frangipani. If I could drive I'd have borrowed his car. It's not a country where one finds bicycles lying about in the hedgerows. Perhaps a horse would come past, a wide slow horse with a cowboy already on it, but room for my case and me behind. I hobbled along the road to the right in what I hoped was the direction of the town. I heard Bob calling... It sounded close so he must be calling me, not Grandma, now. I nipped into the next garden gate and crouched down by the wall, trying not to spoil a bed of lilies. Her life was not all a bed of lilies. Presently Bob started his car and I saw the lights wander slowly as he turned the wheels searching for me in the bushes and along the side of the road. He drove off to the left, so I started after him slowly, hoping he would keep going and not turn round.

Back at his gate I put my case down and limped in to reassure Grandma. Bob had left all the doors and windows wide open and all the lights on. I found her room easily by the sickly mood music roaring out of it. She was sitting up in bed stuffing cotton wool into her ears under her blue rinse and swearing:

'To hell with the younger generation!'

'I'm with you,' I yelled, above the music, and that goes for delicious dish Patsy, too.

'And who the devil are you?'

'I was talking to Bob downstairs.'

'That boy's no good. He's not capable of anything but talk. Can't even get his lips in position without a whole orchestra to back him up. Take my word for it, you're flogging a dead horse there.'

'I wanted to thank you for my supper.'

'Very civil of you. No need to shout ... I'm not deaf.' She took out one piece of cotton wool.

I turned down the mood music.

'Shall I get the Western again for you? Bob's gone out.'

'The original idiot boy. It's fortunate America has a widespread academic organization. In any primitive tribe he'd be the first to starve.'

'He cooks all right.'

'Yes, but he'd never catch anything to cook. I don't suppose you can find it now.'

I twiddled a few knobs and passing through Harold Lloyd and Sonja Henje I arrived at the Alamo.

'God knows what his mother did to him. Did you leave any scotch? He pinched my only bottle. Can't even provide his own liquor. On the rocks!' she called after me as I went down to get it. 'Bring up a bowl of ice with it.'

When I came back into the room she had put on her bifocals and gave me a keen visual going over.

'What on earth is a pretty young woman

like you doing wasting time with our nearest and dearest eunuch anyway?'

'Oh, surely not,' I protested. 'Isn't he just shy? A real American gentleman. I was particularly struck by his kindness.'

She gave a snort and bubbled into her whisky.

'His father was killed in Manila and his grandfather died at Château-Thierry. They'd both turn in their bloody graves to see what the family had come to now. Don't judge America by him, he's the tail end of a good line gone bad.'

'I really think you are being a little hard on your grandson. If I'd been free he might have tried more than he did to...'

'Any man worth his salt tries for any attractive woman whatever the circumstances. Don't tell me you don't know that.'

'Not where I come from, they don't ... anyway, he was doing pretty well ... I didn't help ... for all I know he'd have got around to it later.'

'A slight disorder in the dress is the most you can hope for. He never takes a girl out to dinner unless she's safely married, let alone brings her back for a bit of necking. He makes me sick. What's he doing following *me* about down here? I take off two thousand miles to get away from him and his goddam mother and next thing I know he's back on my doorstep. He's turning into a positive

Proust with this unhealthy grandmother fix-
ation.'

'I should have thought it quite natural to
look up a spirited grandmother once a year,
and not a bit fixated.'

'Let him stick to his mother. I can't be
bothered with him.'

'Poor boy.'

'*Boy* indeed! ... he's thirty-five and looks
more. If he hangs about down here for long
he'll spoil my chances.'

'*Chances?*' I could not help looking surprised.

'Yes, chances ... what's so odd about that?
I can pass myself off as sixty if he doesn't
come drooling round making me go to bed
early.'

'I'm so sorry ... it must have been all my
fault. Do get up again now he's gone.'

She held out her glass to be re-filled,
keeping her eye on the galloping horses.

'Forget it ... I'm comfortable. Do you
know my father came from Wisconsin in a
covered dish?'

'Really?'

'See what I mean about the stock soften-
ing?'

'Perhaps if Bob gets married it'll make a
man of him?'

'Never will.'

'He is considering it now ... he told me.
Then his son may rebel and turn the gener-

ations round again.'

'I'd better make haste with my own wedding then, if the ghastly future you predict lies in wait for me. The Colonel may swallow a grandson ... provided he never sees him ... but a tough with sideboards lisping "great-grandma"...'

'Who's the Colonel?'

'He's a *really* fine American gentleman. Good shot, too. Had to tell him I was laid up with a migraine tonight. Otherwise he might have dropped by and shot the lad.'

'I'm sure if you confide all these problems to Bob he'll move on quick as you could wish.'

'If he's not off first thing in the morning I'll have to...'

'Look, I'm afraid I must go now ... before he comes back. I don't want to see him again.'

'Thought you were stopping the night?'

'It doesn't seem a very good idea any longer.'

'Now don't let me put you off ... depends on what you are after... Dead loss from one point of view ... told you that just now, but it's a good bed. A girl comes in in the morning to make my coffee and check if I've died in my sleep, make you some, too, I dare say.'

'What I'm really after is a lift to the bus station.'

'Call a cab.'

She waved a hand at the telephone beside her bed, and gave me a number. I arranged to be picked up at once.

'Pity you have to go,' she said as I went to the door. 'I have an idea we might have been friends.'

'Any time you are driving through Cardiff...'

'You ought to get that ankle seen to. What did the mouse man do to it? I didn't know he had the strength.'

I sat on my case by the gate waiting for the taxi and praying that Bob would stay down town till I escaped. The people in the house opposite were having a party, spilling out into their garden screaming and scuffling. My head ached now as well as my ankle. Splash, went a merry guest into the pool. I wished it were me. My cool bath lay many hours away. I felt sticky all over and something was biting my wrists, probably a tsetse fly. But it wasn't for long, the taxi arrived after ten minutes and for the brief ride I had a safe place of my own.

That's what I've missed most this last month, my own kitchen. A safe place to go in and out for cups of tea and coffee and eggs and bacon any time, and a day to make pastry, and Bob was right – I wanted to bake cakes for Giorgio and ham in cider and even, without being too ambitious, fresh toast...

But once it comes to cocoa at bedtime the desperation is out of romance and how can anyone sustain illicit romance at all without desperation? I remember they told us at college cocoa was an aphrodisiac but I've never found any truth in that old wives' tale. You must have a talent for adultery like everything else. And a very special talent, a capacity for growing and flowering anywhere. I should never have tried to bring my character and my old life and the *spectre de la cuisine* along with me. If you want to behave light, travel light. Don't clutter yourself up with preconceived ideas, strong-principled husbands, a frantic need to understand, a compulsive puritan tendency to compare, to grade and to improve. Only lie in your hair and your hopeful skin and enjoy the passing butterflies. That's what I'll tell my daughter, and if you can't do that, if you are built for fidelity and mending socks, stay out of it. Stay home and mind the marmalade.

Oh, I was so calm and sensible at last going into the bus station where it was not a bit like the middle of the night. A few people were asleep on the benches, but only sitting up with their heads nodding, not stretched out properly. The others were drinking, eating, reading newspapers, walking round under a steely light, while every now and again the loudspeaker brought in, or sent out, another bus load.

I found I had enough money to get back as far as Kansas City, where I would have to cash travellers cheques to cover the rest of the journey. Kansas City will do for a start. That will be all of a thousand miles away, my bonny lies over the prairie, he lies in his teeth, wrapped in his long teeth all the better to bite you with.

There is no need for me to go to sleep, the bus will be through in an hour. I can wait in the rest-room, stare at my sweaty, dusty, unknown white face. Poor Grandma, how I must have frightened her, looming silently over the bed, like Ophelia back from the drowning, with my hair slopping to my shoulders. Where have all my hairpins gone? How am I to support the old rivers of night with one kirbygrip? Oh, let it go ... let Rose Williams altogether go ... Delilah's strength was in her hair, too. I can't even get a comb through it, not without breaking, so my hair is full of teeth, long teeth all the better to... Oh, never mind, keep moving along there ... get along, little girlie, get along.

The girl at the next wash-basin looked at me oddly. I must have been muttering. I smiled, she looked frightened. Perhaps even my smile was manic now. She asked if I'd lend her a safety-pin. I regretted I had none, and she hurried out, away from my lunatic gaiety. I tried my smile in the glass ... slightly wolverine, but not bad really. After all, I do

211

have very straight white teeth and very straight black brows, and lashes long enough to curl. Don't I? Yes, I do... Who said? I said, I, Rose Williams, on the edge of my right mind but hanging on by the skin of my long teeth with cramp in the stiff upper lip. Feels like a fish-bone wedged in my heart. How did I get here? What happened? Effect never came orderly after cause, giving does not make loving or mean loving. Oh, Giorgio!

I sat on the rest-room floor, cooler, leaning on the case, keeping myself awake with stabs of misery. My ankle is growing like a mushroom cloud, how will I reach the bus? Who will carry my heart? That's right, lay it on thick, anyone would think there'd been a death in the family, wouldn't they now, to hear you go on like that ... ought to be ashamed of yourself, with all those far away Chinese starving to death, when they aren't busy making bombs. The day any recording angel cake comes to grade unhappiness you'll be low down in the scale, girl. Laugh is what they'll do for you ... laugh ... setting up for an international *femme fatale,* a travelling pompadour. You ought to know your place better. Maybe the home class structure's crumbling but whatever made you think you could just walk into the higher echelons of sex and make yourself at home?

Look at you now, in the early stages of schizophrenia, hopping like an old crow with elephantiasis, with your big red angora eyes and your dirty wild hair... Oh, thank you very much... Yes, it is rather heavy... The Kansas City coach? This one? I can manage the step ... I think... Oh, thank you again. Is this seat taken? Oh, that, yes... It is rather swollen now, isn't it? I twisted it falling out of a post office. Oh, it's nothing really. I'll get it cut off in New York. I never seem to have enough hairpins. I can't manage my hair, I can't manage myself. I'm too much for myself, I'm too much for everybody... No room in my skin, as a matter of fact. It's the way my head aches. Oh, I'd love an aspirin, you are kind, I've finished my own... People are so kind, so kind. It's amazing really. All strangers, too. No, you *must* keep the little pillow, I really couldn't take that from you, Mrs Barlow. I saw the name on the label on your little basket. Little baskets are very handy, aren't they? Somehow a girl with a little basket is never without a friend, it's as good as a dog, I don't know why. So many things I don't know why. Oh, please, Mrs Barlow. It isn't that I don't think it's a very *nice* little cushion and it was very clever of your daughter to knit it for you and pink is practically my favourite colour. Oh, well, if you absolutely insist, it *is* more comfortable like that. Thank you. I'm not long for this world, anyway. I mean, it won't be for long, I have to get out at Kansas City. Off in three minutes, are we? Good, the sooner we leave the better. Oh, no, I mean I think your city's fine, *very* fine, oh, of course, the Spanish governor's palace is splendid, you are very lucky to live there ... I mean here ... I'd just love to live there ... I mean here, too, if it weren't that I already live somewhere else. I just happen to live in Wales, *pays de Galles*... Yes, that's right, Prince Charles, too, but we don't see much of him. They've got him in school now, you know ... I've got nothing *against* Santa Fé, nothing at all, it's only that I hurt myself there ... it was all my own fault, no nonsense about fate being against me or heredity or environment or climate, but it hurts just the same. Who's waving? You say somebody's waving for *me*? But I don't have any friends in Santa Fé. Where?

I pushed across poor Mrs stout kind Barlow and her basket to the blue window and fought it open to let in the unwelcome hot night. Giorgio came shouting out of the glass doors of the station disguised as a military policeman with a big white helmet.

He scrabbled against the door of the bus, but the bus was full, the engine running and the door finally hermetically closed.

'Rose!' he yelled. 'Rose ... don't leave me.'

'Better this way.'

'That bad man, that Ted ... I told you ... he has nearly killed me – look!'

I looked. It was a bandage, not a helmet, and right down over one eye, too.

'Does it hurt?'

'*Terrible* ... my whole head ... I have stitches even. Get out at once and look after me!'

'No, I can't–'

'I have been three hours in the hospital. I was not conscious and when I am coming around I don't know where you are for the telephone.'

'You tried to telephone?'

'Of course ... but how? not knowing the name of that awful place?'

'But you did try – you thought about me?'

'I am going nearly out of my mind ... she will be so worried for me, I think, poor girl, with her deep love she will think me dead all this time. I must find her.'

'So what did you do?'

'After more long time they let me go and I am taking a taxi up and down for one hour till I find at last the Swiss chalets, then again I have to take a taxi here. You are a very expensive woman.'

'I'm sorry, Giorgio. That I never meant to be. But I suppose under every housewife's apron beats a mink bikini.'

'You want a mink now, too? and in this terrible weather? What is the matter with you? Why did you not come with me to the hospital? I needed you very badly. What are you doing in there?'

'Going away, Giorgio, dear.'

'But why? Why?'

'To recover.'

'But what shall I do without you?'

The bus began to back out of the yard with Giorgio running alongside, holding on to his bandage.

'But, Rose, I don't understand. Where are you going?'

'New York.'

'Then put your hair up, you are a mess.'

'Yes, Giorgio.'

'How shall I ever sleep without you?'

'Oh, darling – take aspirins ... several.'

'The moment I come in the door he is waiting for me. I had no warning even, I could only say, "Patsy ... Rose says this is your little basket," when he bashed me down flat on the floor ... bang – flat!'

'Poor Giorgio.'

'It was not a fair fight.'

'Poor Giorgio.'

'You should protect me from these savage Americans.'

'Not me. Somebody else.'

'There is nobody else. You should be patient.'

Now he stood away ... farther and farther away, his mouth open still, holding his head, not running any more.

'Giorgio ... it's too late.'

Getting smaller and smaller and darker and whiter and maybe he said he loved me, and maybe he wanted my address, but I couldn't hear another word.

I shut the window and fell back into the air-conditioning to sleep all night on grand-mother Barlow's dreamless shoulder.

Prologue

New York is a very beautiful city. I didn't notice it last time, so much water, so much sky, so many people. Kind, talkative people. Your policemen are wonderful ... hold up all the traffic for me, find me taxis ... everyone served in Europe or vacationed in Europe or hopes to vacation in Europe soon. It seems that what I am, after all, is not a wife or a teacher or a tourist but a European. The elevator man at Rockefeller Center went to Abergavenny to visit his Aunt Gwen ... the girl in Bloomingdales who wrapped the fluffy blue rabbit for Morgan's nephew did the Italian lakes last year and had two days in Rome. That's two more than I ever had. Next year I'll visit Rome, too. Perhaps not next year, but sometime. The doctor who bound so gently my ankle planned to take his wife to Paris in the spring. I won't go to Paris next spring but sometime soon. The buildings and the sidewalks sweated in a grey heat beyond anything I ever experienced, but in the indoor cool I had eight million friends. I loved them all. I loved everybody ... even the hungry bomb-besotted Chinese.

And now on the boat there is too much water. Don't look out of the porthole, don't look over the side to see it rocking, sliding, curling away and down and beyond for ever. My bonny lies over the ocean both ways forward and back. But it's this time I'm going to a New World, a new world of small mortgaged house and small beaten garden and guinea pigs and a pussy cat, and safety-pins and bassinets, because I'm bringing my husband a present from America, an unusual, specially wrapped gift, a brand new fighter (with a Roman nose) for international law and home rule for Wales.

And pray God Morgan's not in jail already when I get home or I don't know whatever I'll tell the woman downstairs as the stout months come round.

The publishers hope that this book has given you enjoyable reading. Large Print Books are especially designed to be as easy to see and hold as possible. If you wish a complete list of our books please ask at your local library or write directly to:

Magna Large Print Books
Magna House, Long Preston,
Skipton, North Yorkshire.
BD23 4ND

This Large Print Book, for people
who cannot read normal print,
is published under the auspices of

THE ULVERSCROFT FOUNDATION

G